lulu in HONOLULU

Elisabeth Wolf

sourcebooks
jabberwocky

To Philip and Emmeline, who make being a mother the most magnificent gift in the world

Copyright © 2014 by Elisabeth Wolf
Cover and internal design © 2014 by Sourcebooks, Inc.
Cover and interior illustrations © Angela Martini

Sourcebooks and the colophon are registered trademarks of Sourcebooks, Inc.

Published by Sourcebooks Jabberwocky, an imprint of Sourcebooks, Inc.
P.O. Box 4410, Naperville, Illinois 60567-4410
(630) 961-3900
Fax: (630) 961-2168
www.jabberwockykids.com

Library of Congress Cataloging-in-Publication data is on file with the publisher.

Source of Production: Versa Press, East Peoria, Illinois, USA
Date of Production: June 2014
Run Number: 5001881

Printed and bound in the United States of America.

VP 10 9 8 7 6 5 4 3 2 1

Prologue:

Lulu's Beginning

ME

Seems like I'm the world's most freckled fish out of water. My mom, dad, and sister suspect that I hatched somewhere far, far away and the stork accidentally dropped me at the wrong doorstep. I'm sure of it. My family is glamorous and fashionable. The Harrisons are Hollywood royalty, even here in Hawaii. The problem is: I'm the coconut that fell far from the tree.

My name is Lulu Harrison, and I'm the eleven-year-old daughter of the massively hot action star Lincoln Harrison and his picture-perfect wife and film director, Fiona. I'm little sister to the cool and trend-obsessed sixteen-year-old Alexis. Of course, I usually live in L.A., entertainment capital of the world, but this summer my address is 1500 Diamond Head Road, Honolulu, Hawaii. My mother is directing and my father is starring in a movie called *Seas the Day*. They are filming right here in O'ahu, Hawaii.

I bet you think I'm gonna have the family vacation of a lifetime, right? Wrong! The problem is: I snorkel, and they sunbathe. I comb the beaches looking for shells. They comb their hair looking great for parties. I'm learning to hula. They're learning to hurry in the MOST laid-back state in the whole United States. Are you starting to understand?

MY FAMILY

Here's what it means to be a fish out of water...

My dad charms everyone, even if they've only read about him in celebrity magazines. So you can imagine how much he dazzles me! He's a mega-cool, real-life Prince Charming. Since we've been in Hawaii, his deep green eyes have greened deeper because his face is all tan and his thick brown hair lightened from the sun. But I have this suspicion that my dad has NO idea what could happen to MY skin in the sun. I'm totally convinced that he has no clue what I do in O'ahu all day or whether I've even made a friend.

My mom stands tall and acts regal. All those Hawaiian queens and princesses would have lots in common with my mother, Fiona. Proud. In charge. Confident. Super busy. Naturally good at giving orders. Being a queen and being a director could be, like, the same job. I don't like being a subject though. I struggle to measure up.

My sister, Alexis, thinks volcanoes must have erupted fifty million years ago just to make the Hawaiian islands for her. Hawaii is a paradise for girls like my sister who look perfect in every cut, color, and combination of bikini ever sold. Her long, twig-sized legs and matching twig arms are baked to a golden brown. She shakes her silky black hair to a seemingly constant rhythm only she hears. People keep asking her if she's a model. She loves that beyond words.

Here's how I look in Hawaii: like a beekeeper. My skin is like a patch of snow with a few sixteen-ounce bags of chocolate chips scattered on top. I have to cover up completely or else my pasty-white skin burns, blisters, and becomes miserable. Once the lobster-red color fades, I'm left with thousands of new freckles. The hot, tropical, salty air has caused my unruly, frizzy hair to double in size. There's no brush that would want to go near it. Alexis says I'm going to end up with dreadlocks if I don't get my hair under control. Personally, I think my pale, freckled body—that has added a few pounds thanks to my delicious coconut milk shakes—would go great with brown dreadlocks. And, of course, the Hawaiian version of me with the dreads would still have my greeny eyes, curious brain, and real feelings.

THE REAL LULU

In case you secretly believe being a kid in the world of moviemakers can be fun, DON'T! Because here's what being different means:

1. In a surf store, I tried to buy two bars of lychee nut soap. When the checkout guy asked what kind of board I had, Alexis laughed so hard she almost fainted. What I thought was good smelling natural soap was warm-water surfboard wax.

2. Alexis commands me to wear flip-flops to the beach or else she won't take me. I can't walk in flip-flops. My toes curl over the tops, and if I'm lucky, I only trip.

3. When the super-famous, super-skinny lead actress in my mom's new movie came to dinner, there was a Japanese feast and only chopsticks to eat it with. Every morsel I grabbed or stabbed slid everywhere except into my mouth. When a dumpling I thought I had secured went *splat* onto the actress's toe, my mother excused me from dinner.

4. As soon as I landed in Honolulu, my mom's assistant, who's in L.A., signed me up for stand-up paddle board camp. Problem is: I can't stand up. I fall. I can't paddle on my knees either. I fall. If I sit on the board and there aren't any waves, I don't fall. But, well, there are always waves in the ocean. I changed camps.

Here's what I feel like: the Pua 'ilima, a small plant with fuzzy leaves, with a yellow-orangey five-petal flower that blooms on the end of short, green stems. The Pua 'ilima happens to be O'ahu's island flower and grows everywhere from the mountains to the seashore. Even though millions of tourists visit O'ahu, Hawaii's most popular island, none of them would say they come for the Pua 'ilima. They notice the splashy, flashy parts of

O'ahu, like the giant waves; white, powdery sand beaches; deep green mountains taller than the Alps; black-brown scratchy lava rocks; and bold red hibiscus. But this summer, the Harrisons are going to realize that tough plant with the orange flowers has something special. Oh, and just so you know, the Pua 'ilima symbolizes LOVE. Perfect-o!

THE NEW LULU

At the end of the summer, my family will pack up and head home to Los Angeles, back to the same old place where you can't see the stars in the night sky, dogs and Frisbees aren't allowed on the beaches, and my parents are too busy making movies to make time to be a family. Well, that's what's incredible about this summer. Family life in Honolulu isn't like family life in L.A. Alexis and I flew to Hawaii with my parents for our first-ever family summer vacation. Here's how it works: my parents spend time with my sister and me every afternoon and evening between 4 p.m. and 8 p.m. That might sound crazy, to have your family time scheduled like that, but for me it's HUGE. Small problem, though, is when I need my parents for something not between the hours of four and eight. Ya see, my day camp is trying to win an island-wide hula competition, but it's during the day. My parents will absolutely, positively come watch me—even if it takes a little eruption to get them there.

Because movies and TV shows are always being made in Hawaii, I'm going to write my story as my own screenplay. Here's the title: *Lulu in Honolulu*. Geez peas! That has a good ring to it, right? Besides, you'd be surprised how many people in Hawaii say they're writing a script (starting with the Hawaiian Airlines flight attendant on our plane).

So I'm going to write my parents a new screenplay starring

people they know and love. And who knows? They may realize I'm a little coconut that didn't fall THAT far from the tree.

So, roll OPENING CREDITS…

LULU IN HONOLULU

BY LULU HARRISON

ACT 1: SHAKE IT TILL YOU MAKE IT

SCENE 1: HULA FOR BEGINNERS

EXT. WAIMANALO BEACH PARK, GRASSY AREA UNDER TREES—MONDAY MIDMORNING

 CUT!! Hey, just so you know, I've written a screenplay once before. It was about my life in L.A. So I'm getting the hang of it. In case this is the first screenplay you've ever read, here's some script lingo you should know. Before each scene, I'll write where it's happening. If I put "EXT" that means what's gonna happen is outside or "exterior." If I put "INT" that means what's gonna happen is inside or "interior." Most of the other stuff you'll get just because you've probably seen movies or TV shows. What I'm writing is like what actors and directors read before they film a movie. OK, back to: ACTION!!

FADE IN ON:

A tattered blue flag that says "OHANA DAY CAMP" whips

back and forth in the wind. It's stuck between the slats of a wooden picnic table.

The hot, bright summer sun filters down through tree limbs. The patchy sunlight falls on twelve kids ranging in age from eight to fourteen. They shuffle, stamp, turn, and wiggle in two horizontal lines. All wear bathing suits and are barefoot except one. LULU, an eleven-year-old girl, thrusts her hips from side to side as she tries to follow the movements of the girl in front of her. Clothing covers her from head to toe. Her enormous swarm of brown hair is mashed under a white and red baseball cap that says "ALOHA," but the "O" is shaped like a heart colored in with a rainbow. AUNTIE MOANA, an older Hawaiian woman with short black hair and warm cocoa-colored eyes that match her skin, softly calls out movements as she herself does them.

AUNTIE MOANA

One, two, three, tap. Sway. Sway. Sway. One, two three, tap. Sway. Sway.

A man, UNCLE AKAMU, with salt-and-pepper hair, strums a ukulele as he watches the waves crashing onto the beach behind the dancers.

AUNTIE MOANA
(to kids in the back rows)

Follow the person in front of you if you're lost.
(to all the kids)
And...step up, forward. Step up, back.

LULU
(slightly out of breath)
I'm so lost I don't know forward from backward.

Next to Lulu in the back row, NOELANI, a slim girl about Lulu's age, slides her feet and floats her arms to the hula music. Her rhythm and motions are one with the breezes blowing through the trees and the waves washing onto the shore. She wears a stretched-out tankini top and board shorts that have faded from blue to almost gray. Noelani's long, black braid hangs down her back and thwacks her brown shoulders as she turns from side to side.

NOELANI
(giggles)
Lu, forward is what's in front of your nose.

Lulu looks up from her feet and watches KHLOE. Khloe's smooth waving arms and swaying match the ukulele's melody. And even though the wind blows her long, straight blond hair, not a strand looks out of place. She wears a skimpy leopard bikini with pink straps.

LULU
(quietly to Noelani)
Khloe better be right in front of me at the hula-off next week or else I'm gonna mess up a zillion times.

Uncle Akamu finishes the song, HUKILAU. Auntie Moana lightly claps to get the children's attention.

CUT!! Scripts don't usually do this, but I have to break into the story to tell you something Hawaiian. Auntie Moana isn't really my aunt or an aunt to anyone at Ohana Camp. All us kids just call her Auntie. One thing I love about Hawaii is that Hawaiians treat neighbors, friends, and even friends of friends as part of their family. *Ohana* means "family" in Hawaiian. And, in Hawaii, you call someone Auntie and Uncle if they're older than you. It's a sign of respect. Auntie Moana was born in Hawaii, in the same house in the Waimanalo neighborhood where she lives now. And wanna know something else cool? Her name means "ocean" and her husband, Akamu, his name means "earth." Uncle Akamu told us kids that he knew Moana would complete his life the moment they met 'cause they would be the perfect joining of the earth and the sea. Wow! Now, that's so much more romantic than any gross, kissy stuff my sister Alexis thinks is love. OK, now back to: ACTION!!

AUNTIE MOANA
(addresses all the kids)
Before we do the dance again...

Several children groan.

AUNTIE MOANA
(ignoring them)
...let's remind each other about hula basics.

KHLOE
(jumping right in)

The movements should be smooth and delicate. And our feet do something different than our arms so, like, arms and feet go in different directions.

> LULU
> (out loud)
> Geez peas! No wonder I mess up. I have a hard enough time getting my arms and feet to go in the same direction.

Campers around her crack up. Uncle Akamu winks at her.

> KHLOE
> And our hips never stop moving while our upper body...

> AUNTIE MOANA
> *Mahalo*, Khloe. Thank you. Anyone else?

CAROLE, a skinny, tall girl with deep black hair and eyes, wearing a tiny leopard-print bikini, yells out.

> CAROLE
> Hands and arms tell the story.

> AUNTIE MOANA
> Yes, *mahalo*. Hands and arms paint the picture.

CATE, a petite blond wearing the same leopard bikini as Carole, leaves her line and walks up near Lulu.

> CATE
> Always be on your flat feet. And...

>   (looks down at Lulu's orange-and-white checkered
>   Van's shoes)
> ...hula is performed barefoot.

                          LULU
Well, I just don't want to burn the tops of my feet.

                     AUNTIE MOANA
Keiki, children, there is something important you are
not yet telling me.

No one says anything. LIAM and MALEKO, two tall boys, flick
each other's arms as they goof around.

Noelani clears her throat. Lulu turns to look at her. She's never
heard her best pal speak up in the group before. Noelani mostly
saves her ideas and her jokes to share with Lulu.

                       NOELANI
Ummmm. *Kumu?*

Hearing her friend use the Hawaiian word for teacher, Lulu
smiles. Noelani knows so much stuff, but she's SO quiet about it.

Noelani hesitates, nervous now that everyone in the class is
looking at her.

                          LULU
Hey, what were ya gonna say?

Noelani looks down at her bare feet.

LULU
(in a loud voice)
I bet you were gonna say that the most important part of
dancing hula is not to look at me, so I don't mess you up.

All the kids giggle, except Khloe, Cate, and Carole, who call
themselves KHLOE AND THE Cs. They exchange glances.

Noelani lifts her eyes from the ants crawling over her left toe.
She finds courage in Lulu's clowning.

NOELANI
I think the most important part of performing hula
is akua.

Uncle Akamu continues to look out at the surf, but his brown
eyes crinkle in the corners, his way of smiling.

Auntie Moana takes a moment to answer. She pauses—not
like she's thinking, more like she's listening to the wind and a
message it's sending through the trees.

AUNTIE MOANA
Mahalo, Noelani. Yes, akua. Spirit. That's the only way to
dance hula. You must feel the akua.

Uncle Akamu plays the hula music again.

The kids shuffle into the starting hula stance: knees slightly bent
and heels together.

Lulu looks down at her feet.

AUNTIE MOANA

OK, feel the music.

LULU
(talking to herself, but loud enough for all around her
to hear)

Right, together. Right, tap. Left, together. Left, tap.

AUNTIE MOANA

Now sway, sway, sway.

Suddenly, a LOUD VOICE SCREECHES from the parking lot.

LOUD VOICE

KHLOE!! KHHHHLLLOOOEEE! CAROLE and CAAATE!!!!

SCENE 2: NO MORE FOLLOW THE LEADER

EXT. WAIMANALO BEACH PARK—CONTINUOUS

Uncle Akamu continues to strum the *hukilau* on his ukulele. The kids and Auntie Moana stamp, flutter, and rock to and fro.

The calling of KHHLOOOE, CAROLE, and CAAAATE gets louder. Khloe's mother, MRS. CLARISSA LYONS, wearing tight pink pants and matching pink lipstick, approaches the Ohana Camp flag.

Khloe and the Cs break ranks and scramble over to Mrs. Lyons.

MRS. LYONS
(to Khloe and the Cs)
You're in. Now, hurry. Get your stuff.

Khloe and the Cs dash off to grab their beach bags and flip-flops.

The music comes to an end. Ohana Camp kids drift over to Khloe and the Cs, but no one knows what to say. Well, except one.

LULU
What's going on? Where are you guys going?

Khloe tosses her plush pink towel around her neck. Lulu notices that "KHLOE" is embroidered on the towel in red and that Cate and Carole have the same towel with their names stitched on.

KHLOE
(squealing with delight)
We're going to the very best-est dance school, Island School of Hula!

CATE
So we're gonna be on the team that wins the hula-off.

CAROLE

And we'll perform onstage at the Ala Moana Center all during the summer.
                    (squeals excitedly)
And we'll win the prize money too.

Lulu tugs her long-sleeved sun-protection shirt so that she's covered all the way to her wrists.

LULU

I wish you guys weren't leaving. Today I brought taro chips and my homemade mango salsa. I wanna share it with everyone.

At the mention of salsa, the redheaded twin sister and brother, KENNA and KAPONO, perk up.

KENNA

Ohhh. Can I try if it's not really spicy?

KAPONO

I want it to be extra spiced!

LULU
                    (to Kenna and Kapono)
You'll both have to try it and tell me what ya think.
                    (to Khloe and the Cs)
I spent lots of time making the salsa. You guys are gonna miss it.

KHLOE

Well, maybe instead of wasting time chopping up mangos, you should work on your hula.

KHLOOOOOE, CAROLE, and CAAAATE cut through the warm beachy air.

Carole and Cate scamper toward the parking lot. Khloe pauses to put her feet in her rose-colored flip-flops.

NOELANI
(softly so that she can barely be heard)
Hey, good luck, Khloe. You're a great dancer.

KHLOE

You too, Noelani.

Khloe runs to catch up to Carole and Cate.

SCENE 3: GOTTA WIN ONE

EXT. ON WAIMANALO BEACH—FIVE MINUTES LATER

Waimanalo's smooth sand bakes in the midday sun. Rough waves fling tropical-green and sapphire-blue water onto the shore, where it turns quickly to bubbly, white foam. The beach is quiet. Other than the Ohana Camp kids, there aren't many others around.

Lulu and Noelani sit next to each other on a straw mat. Lulu's under an orange beach umbrella. She peels away big, damp leaves, the wrapping for what looks like a meatball, and takes a bite. Noelani studies a Hawaiian language workbook.

Lulu waves the half-eaten ball in Noelani's direction.

> LULU
> (with mouth full)
> Sure you don't want any *laulau*?

> NOELANI
> (looks up)
> OK.

Lulu hands Noelani her piece. Suddenly Kapono pelts Noelani with a WET SAND BALL. It EXPLODES on her book.

> LULU and NOELANI
> Hey!

> LULU
> (to Noelani)
> Maybe Kapono could ruin *my* Hawaiian workbook. I'm terrible at learning Hawaiian. How can a language that only has twelve letters be soooooo complicated?

> NOELANI
> It's not hard, especially for me, 'cause I grew up hearing it.

> LULU
> Maybe it's hard 'cause of all those vowels.

NOELANI
(laughing)
Hawaiian has the same vowels as English.

LULU
Then maybe only having seven consonants makes all those vowels too much for my mouth.

Noelani rolls out from under the shade of the mat into the hot sunshine.

NOELANI
Here's a good word for the day: *koa*.

LULU
Does it mean: give me more *laulau*?

NOELANI
It means brave.

LULU
Cool. Did you just learn that?

NOELANI
I was just thinking about it, Lu. I really, really hoped we'd win the hula-off. Now, without Khloe and the Cs, there's no way.

LULU
(puts her ALOHA cap on and sticks her head outside
the umbrella)

Noelani, you're a super-looper, better hula dancer than all of them put together.

NOELANI
(softly, barely heard over the waves)
I have no *koa*. I'm too scared to dance in front of anyone. And a huge crowd? That's totally impossible.

LULU
So don't worry about it. We'll all just go to the hula-off for fun. I really hope my parents might come.

NOELANI
(stares at Lulu)
I just thought, if we win, Ohana Camp could get the prize money.

Kenna runs over to Lulu and Noelani. Tears stream down her face. A gaggle of boys, led by Kapono, follows behind her.

KAPONO
We didn't do anything!

KENNA
(yelling in her loudest little-girl voice)
YES, you did. I have sand in my hair and all over.

The boys and Kenna scooch onto Lulu's mat. They all try to explain what happened.

NOELANI
(in her soft voice)
Well, just forget it. We should all just get along, like one big *ohana*.

LULU
Geez peas! Instead of sand fights, why don't we do something together, like win that hula competition? Wouldn't that be an awesome shock and surprise for Khloe and the Cs and the kids at Island School of Hula?

NOELANI
(turns to Lulu)
That's not too nice.

KAPONO
(waving his foot in the air)
Yeah! Let's kick their butts!

Lulu jumps up, almost hitting her head on her umbrella.

LULU
Well, I'm in.

Kenna giggles and totally forgets about her sandy hair.

KENNA
That's so funny, Lulu, 'cause you're like the worst hula-er ever!

SCENE 4: HOME ON THE LANAI

EXT/INT. HARRISON FAMILY HOUSE, DIAMOND HEAD—ONE HOUR LATER

CUT!! Again. You should know about this house we're living in for the summer. It's in my mom and dad's contract that the studio has to rent them a big, fancy house while they are making a movie. This house has lots of sliding glass walls that stay open all day long. So, even though you're inside, you feel like you're outside at the same time. The only problem is that Watson, our chubby pug, crashes into the glass. He can't figure out the difference between inside and outside.

Here's what I like about this house: I can see the ocean from every room. Here's what I don't like: there's nowhere I could munch a Nanea Hawaiian chocolate macadamia nut bar without leaving brown flecks. The floors are whitewashed wood and covered with a giant pale wool rug. Low, cushy couches are a color called *sand*, which is crazy because specks of sand aren't allowed in this hyper-clean place. Walls that aren't glass are painted Tibetan Jasmine, and I know that because my mother insisted on having them repainted before we moved in. In nooks and corners of the house stand dark wooden sculptures that you can't sneeze near because they're precious Tahitian antiques. Oh, and in case you thought you could prop up your feet, DON'T! The tables are made of glass. OK, back to: ACTION!!

Lulu, sandy and sweaty from a day of Ohana Camp, dashes through the house's large, two-story-high double doors. She almost trips on WATSON, who lies on the natural bamboo doormat. Watson has chewed through three of the four corners. He loves chomping the mat because it feels like he's chewing a stick without him actually needing to find or fetch one himself.

MAYA, a tall, older woman with dark skin and blue eyes, lifts her right hand to form a STOP sign. She doesn't need to say a word. Her thin hand and long fingers command immediate attention.

 CUT!! Quick important information I want you to know. Maya moved to Hawaii from Japan when she was eight years old. When I first met her, I thought she didn't like me because she doesn't chitchat, but I learned that her kindness runs deep and that just because she doesn't blab doesn't mean she doesn't listen! She takes care of our house, which also means she helps take care of me. Back to: ACTION!!

LULU

Aloha, Maya. I know. Shoes. Off.

Lulu plops onto the front doorstep and kicks off her sand-filled checkered Vans. Maya smiles. Her face easily creases in places it has folded many times before.

Walking out the front door, ALEXIS looks down at Lulu. Alexis carries an ISLAND LIFE magazine. Wearing a black string bikini top, a wide-brimmed white sun hat, and tiny white shorts printed with black stars, Alexis looks as if she just walked out of a page in the magazine.

LULU

I gotta talk to Mom and Dad. It's mega important hula business.

ALEXIS
(barely hiding a smile)
Since when are you a hula star?

LULU

I'm NOT. That's especially why they've gotta come to the hula-off.

Alexis pulls Lulu's hands to help her up.

LULU

Lex. Seriously. If they'd come watch me, it would be like a dream come true. They've never been to any show or program I've been in at school.

ALEXIS
(trying to keep a laugh out of her voice)
Lu, I'm serious. If your thing is during the day, there's about as much chance of them coming as there is of it snowing in Honolulu.

LULU

And there're these girls called Khloe and the Cs who just bailed on dancing with us, so if Mom and Dad came, it could make my friends and me feel fantabulous.

Lulu heads inside the house, but Maya blocks the door. She points a finger toward the outdoor shower. Lulu knows what the finger means: rinse off before you set foot in the most dirt-free, sand-free beach house in all seven Hawaiian Islands.

CAMERA FOLLOWS LULU as she walks around to a wood-slatted wall covered with a Hawaiian wedding flower vine and ducks into the shower. She tugs off her SURF MAUI T-shirt that's over her SPF 50 long-sleeved shirt but stops mid-tug. Just before her head pops out, she yanks her shirt down.

 CUT!! Another super quick note. Even though I couldn't surf if a shark was speeding after me, I love wearing surf shirts because the idea of riding on wave power is, well, soooo Hawaii and California! Now, Back to: ACTION!!

Lulu faintly hears voices drift from the back of the house and takes off toward the *lanai*, the word everyone in Hawaii uses for porch.

LULU
(yelling over the sounds of waves and singing shama thrushes hidden in trees)
Mahhhhhm?! Dahhhhhd?! Are you home already?

FIONA HARRISON stands straight and tall against the *lanai* railing. Her posture and her angular beauty make her seem like a marble statue. She's dressed in narrow white jeans with zippers at the ankles, a plain white top cut high at the neck and a silky Stella McCartney blazer with the sleeves pushed up, showing off her large, rose gold men's watch and gold and diamond bangles. She wears high wedge shoes that are both stylish and professional. Her chestnut brown hair is swept into a neat ponytail. LINCOLN HARRISON lies on a chaise with the back support pulled down flat. He's barefoot and wears only Rip Curl shorts and vintage tortoiseshell Wayfarer sunglasses.

FIONA
(to Linc in an angry tone)
Not only did you act unprofessional on the set today, but you were downright childish!

LINC
(laid-back tone but mad underneath)
You squeezing my scene into only a few takes makes me stress out. All right? I deal with nerves on the set by clowning. Give me a break!

Linc props himself up and sips an icy blue drink with a wedge of pineapple stuck to the side of the glass.

FIONA
(British accent getting more clipped with each word)
You know very well why I'm rushing you. My one-hundred-and-fifty-million-dollar movie production is millions of dollars over budget and weeks behind schedule. Don't you think I...
(imitating Linc's deep voice)
..."stress out"?

Lulu walks onto the *lanai* but is unnoticed by her parents. Alexis drifts outside from the living room. She's careful not to catch her heel in the track where the glass door travels. Watson troops out after her.

FIONA
(sharp tone)
After Lulu's last birthday, we BOTH agreed to take the girls this summer. And we BOTH agreed we'd wrap each day in time to be with the girls by dark.

Lulu and Alexis catch each other's eye. Lulu pulls her ALOHA hat brim over her eyes. It's an instinct to try and hide. Alexis, however, clicks in her high, pointy heels right over to her parents.

ALEXIS
Hi, Fiona and Linc. Lulu here has a *très* important scheduling request.

Fiona immediately spins around and looks at Lulu. She takes a split second to change her tone.

FIONA
Yes, Lulu?! Hi, Lex. We're home extra early today since...ah...

Linc spins a little paper umbrella between his fingers.

LINC
I wasn't having my best day on the *Seas the Day* set.

ALEXIS

Well, Lu, you've got the stage.

Alexis gives Lulu an encouraging wink but also twirls her hand around her wrist indicating Lulu needs to come out with it already.

LULU
(tugs her hat brim up)
I was wondering, and, well, hoping you guys could come to the hula-off. It's this gigantic competition I'm in with my camp friends.

FIONA

A what "off"?

LULU

Hula. We really wanna try to win because whatever group wins gets prize money and performs at Ala Moana Center all summer.

ALEXIS
(smiling)
The biggest, coolest mall in Honolulu? Now I'm totally interested.

LULU
(speaks super fast)
And, geez peas, you guys have never come watch me in anything, ya know. It's what lots of parents do bec—

ALEXIS
(to Fiona)
Seriously, Fiona, it seems Lulu's camp had some girls bail today. If you and Dad show up to support Lu and her hula-dancing pals, that would, well, spread a little Hollywood glam to an otherwise hopeless cause.

FIONA
Look. I get it. But your father and I are stretched very thin. Is it at night? Get the information to Lilac and she'll check.

LULU
Your assistant? But she's in L.A.

FIONA
Yes, Lulu, but I always use the cell phone.

Linc sits up and props his shades on the top of his head.

LINC
You use about six of them, Fiona.

Linc picks up his glass, pulls out the pineapple, and tosses it to the floor. He drains the glass.

LULU
Hey, Dad, gotta be careful about Watson. He could eat anything that's on the ground.

Linc gets up from the chaise.

                          LINC

I'm gonna check the surf before that smelly pug comes
near me.

He passes Lulu, lifts up her ALOHA cap, and musses her
already-wild hair.

                          LINC

    Nice 'do.

Linc heads down to the beach, and Fiona follows in her
high shoes.

                          LULU
                   (calling after him)
    Daaad! We really wanna try and win this hula thing. If
    you'd come, it would inspire us!

WIDE SHOT of Linc halfway to the ocean.

                         ALEXIS
    K. Let's not take their answer as a no.

Watson scrounges around Linc's chair. Lulu reaches down to
pick up the pineapple wedge her dad tossed on the ground just
before the pug chomps down on it.

                          LULU
                (looking up from the ground)
    Of course not. I take it as a solid maybe.

SCENE 5: TOPS AND BOTTOMS

INT. SPLASH! ALA MOANA CENTER—NEXT MORNING

SPLASH! is a Hawaiian swimwear boutique. Bathing suits in all different colors, shapes, and sizes hang throughout the store. Almost every one is a bikini.

Lulu holds up a magenta, fringed bikini top.

LULU

Is this a belt?

ALEXIS

Are you that fashion-challenged or are you trying to be funny?

Alexis's arms hold a dozen bikini tops and bottoms.

SHAWNA, the Splash! manager, casually approaches Alexis. With her gorgeous, wavy, dark hair and deep-brown skin, she looks like she fell off one of the posters of bathing suit models hanging around the store.

SHAWNA

Aloha, Alexis? Right? I'm Shawna. Let me help you with those.

Alexis gratefully releases the tangle of hangers.

Alexis, thrilled to be known by the naturally hip manager of one of O'ahu's coolest swimsuit stores, flashes her violet eyes.

ALEXIS
I totally love the vibe of your store and how you always have the newest styles.

LULU
Aloha, Shawna. I'm her sister, Lulu.

SHAWNA
(warm and welcoming)
Hey, Lulu. Actually, I came over to you guys 'cause I heard you say you thought the knotted fringe top looked like a belt. I thought that was hysterical.

Lulu shoots Alexis an "I told you so" glance.

LULU
You sure sell tiny pieces of material that are supposed to be bathing suits.

Lulu picks up a turquoise twist bandeau top with removable straps and holds it up. She then grabs banded, ruched-side bottoms. Both pieces look especially tiny dangling from their hangers.

LULU
How could anyone wear these into the water? First wave and *adios*, bathing suit.

ALEXIS

Hey, what size are those bottoms? If they're smalls, hand them over. Totally *très* adorable.

Alexis heads toward the small changing-room area and swishes behind a silky drape of blue and green tropical leaves.

SHAWNA
(to Lulu)

Is there anything you need?

ALEXIS
(yelling out from changing room)

Shawna! Can you help Lulu? She needs to win a hula contest and needs something to wear that's not SPF 50 long underwear!

SHAWNA

That's so cool! You hula?

LULU

Well, at Ohana Day Camp, where I go, we're learning all kinds of Hawaiian life and culture stuff, but there's this hula-off coming up and—

SHAWNA

I hula-ed for years before I got into surfing. Let's see your moves! C'mon. I can help you!

Shawna clears away a rack in the middle of the store and positions Lulu's hands and feet into basic hula moves.

> **LULU**
> For me, hula feels more like a game of Twister than a dance.

Shawna cracks up.

> **SHAWNA**
> You might be better at being funny than at hula, Lulu.

Alexis parades out in a Luli Fama Cosita Buena push-up top and Brazilian-back bottoms.

> **ALEXIS**
> (to Shawna)
> Does this look too big?

> **LULU**
> Lex, put something on! Anyone passing the store could see you!

> **SHAWNA**
> (smiling to Alexis)
> She's got a point. Great bikinis don't always make great mall wear.

> **ALEXIS**
> I know, but bikinis are good for hula! Look, how hard can that dancing be?!

Shawna cranks up the store music. Lulu and Alexis shake, sway, twist, stamp, and spin. Shawna instructs in between giggles and joining in herself.

ALEXIS
(still dancing about)
See, Lu, all you need is a bikini to wear for your hula thingy-dingy, and the moves will just flow into you!

Lulu stops mid-twirl. Khloe and the Cs stand staring and sniggering.

LULU
Hey, guys! Just practicing some hula moves because bathing suit shopping is about the worst shopping I can think of, and I don't like shopping to begin with.
(looks at Shawna)
Sorry, Shawna.

SHAWNA
(reaching to turn down the music)
I get it. Bathing suit shopping is known to be stressful for most women.

KHLOE
You weren't shopping, and you weren't doing hula. You were being, like, freaks.

Alexis, despite being clad in a skimpy bathing suit, strides right over to Khloe and the Cs. She shakes back her long, silky hair as she bores her eyes into Khloe.

ALEXIS
Hi. I'm Alexis Harrison.

Khloe and the Cs blush. They are meeting a mega-cool teenager who's actually been photographed in magazines with her famous parents. They stand frozen.

> ALEXIS
>
> K. Let me put it another way. I'm Lulu's big sister.

> KHLOE
>
> Oh. We didn't know that was you.

> ALEXIS
>
> Then, HELLLO?! Who did you think I was?

> LULU
> (jumps in)
>
> No problem. We, I mean, I was just getting super-looper excited about the hula-off.

> ALEXIS
>
> Which, by the way, Lulu's camp...
> (pauses and looks to Lulu)
> What's it called?

> LULU
> (whispering)
>
> Ohana.

> ALEXIS
>
> Fine. Whatever. Ohana Camp is gonna rock that hula show and our parents are gonna make sure of it!

KHLOE

NO way to that. Those misfit kids dancing without me leading them will be a freak show.

Alexis turns and casually shuffles through racks of bathing suits hanging nearby.

SHAWNA
(to Khloe and the Cs)
Did you guys need some help?

KHLOE
We better go. We've got hula practice.

ALEXIS
(under her breath)
You guys are gonna need it.

SCENE 6: FIRST THINGS FIRST

EXT. BACKYARD AND *LANAI* OF AUNTIE MOANA AND UNCLE AKAMU'S HOUSE, WAIMANALO—NEXT MORNING

CUT!! Here's something you need to know about Auntie Moana and Uncle Akamu's house. I LOVE IT. It has a small, square-shaped grass yard. Chickens cluck in a pen. Kittens prowl around looking for someone to stroke them. There's even a white llama who lets you hug her! Ohana Camp meets here on days we have lots of crafts to do and there's too much stuff to lug down the street to the Waimanalo Beach Park or if there's a jellyfish warning and we can't go in the water. OK, back to: ACTION!!

Auntie Moana shows Kenna and Kapono how to make twisted ginger *leis*. Liam teaches himself an easy four-chord Hawaiian melody on his ukulele. Uncle Akamu's sister, CARIDYN, sits on the *lanai* with her large *pahu* drum. She lifts and drops Maleko's hands on the drum, so he hears the different sounds. Noelani sits on a step and lightly shakes bright feathers.

CAMERA pulls back for a WIDE SHOT of Lulu. She wobbles on a folding chair placed up against a tree trunk. The top half of Lulu's body is lost in branches and leaves.

                    LULU
         (voice coming from somewhere in the tree)
There're so many papayas up here. Geez peas! And they
look really big.

                AUNTIE MOANA
         (calling from a bench full flowers)
Good, Lulu. Pick. We'll bake papaya bread this afternoon.

                  NOELANI
              (in her small voice)
Auntie, I thought we had to do hula practice all afternoon?

AUNTIE MOANA

Well, if the papayas are nice and ripe, it's also time for papayas. We have to follow nature to know what time it is.

(calls out to Lulu)

Are the papayas ripe?

LULU

I think so. They're not green at all. And feel really soft and—

Just then a yellow bell-shaped fruit sails to the ground and SPLATS its yellow orange flesh.

LULU

Sorry!

AUNTIE MOANA

Now we know they are perfectly ripe.

Noelani stands. CAMERA FOLLOWS Noelani as she strides across the backyard. Loose stitching from her too-small board shorts float around her legs as she walks.

At the tree, Noelani grabs the back of Lulu's shaky chair.

NOELANI

(up to Lulu)

I thought I'd better steady the chair so you don't smoosh open your head.

LULU

Mahalo. I'd been feeling like I was standing on guava jelly!
Noe, do you have a favorite fruit? Mine's pineapple. But
it's such a hard shape and so prickly, how does anyone
cut it open?

NOELANI

I like coconuts, but they're not really fruit.

Lulu's arms and head appear from the tree. She starts to climb down.

LULU

When I was little, I thought coconuts came from cows
'cause they had milk in them.

Noelani laughs, and it sounds like it comes from deep inside.
Her dark-cocoa eyes sparkle. Lulu giggles.

The THAWP BOOM BOOM of Caridyn's *pahu* drum signals
the kids to gather around Auntie Moana.

AUNTIE MOANA

Only one more day. Right? So, let's practice our hula.

Kids scramble into their usual lines, but with Khloe and the Cs
gone, Lulu now stands front and center.

AUNTIE MOANA

Remember: three basic steps for hula. Start with our
beginning stance. Knees a little bent. Feet in a pie shape.
Then, what's next?

Kids fidget or look down. Some even shift their feet out of the pie-shape starting position.

Caridyn starts drumming to fill the awkward silence.

> CARIDYN
>
> Hey, are you guys dancing the *hukilau*? I still remember how to drum that song. I can even keep time with the gourd. Go on. Let's see this winning group.

> AUNTIE MOANA
>
> What are the other moves for your bottom half? Anyone?

> NOELANI
>
> (softly, barely able to be heard)
>
> *Kaholo* and *'ami.*

Lulu twists around to look at Noelani.

> LULU
>
> Noe?! C'mon. Call it out—

Noelani shakes her head.

> LULU
>
> Geez peas! Why not tell Auntie?

> NOELANI
>
> (whispering back)
>
> I don't want her to put me in the front.

The drumming starts. Lulu tries to figure out the dance, but without anyone in front of her, she's toast!

All the kids shuffle into each other. Some sway backward when they should sway forward. Some arms raise up while others hang down. Kids try to dance their hula but look more like a cross between zombies and bumper cars. The drumming stops. There was nothing award-winning about that performance.

> MALEKO
>
> Hey, guys, that was cruddy. And I don't even know anything about hula. I'd rather drum.

> AUNTIE MOANA
>
> That was hard because we are used to performing with Uncle Akamu's ukulele.

Caridyn points her thumb toward the house.

> CARIDYN
>
> Want me to get Akamu's uke? Ukulele's also a rhythm instrument. I can play one.

> AUNTIE MOANA
>
> Let's go again. If it's drumming, singing, or ukulele, doesn't matter. It's your akua. Your spirit. How you feel inside.

Auntie Moana takes a slow, deep breath.

AUNTIE MOANA

Noelani, come be the pelican who flies in front of the flock. Lead them where to go.

Noelani cannot move. She examines her toes. All the Ohana kids turn and look at her.

SCREEN DOOR SLAMS. Uncle Akamu jumps the three steps from the *lanai* to the grass.

UNCLE AKAMU

Stop, *keiki*! Hold up. We gotta get to Lanikai Beach. There's a monk seal pup hauled out on the sand. We need to make sure no one disturbs that sleeping pup. There're no other volunteers around.

Uncle Akamu runs toward his dented, scratched, blue van. His keys jangle from a stretchy band around his wrist. Kids race after him. Lulu, despite running as gracefully as a seal on sand, reaches the van before the other kids.

 CUT!! This is mega important about the Hawaiian monk seal. Their real, Hawaiian name is *Ilio-holo-i-ka-uaua*. Don't ask me to ever say it, but it means "dog that runs in rough water." They're supposed to be protected from being hurt or hunted, but their population is still going down. Monk seals are native to Hawaii, and that means they're not found anywhere else in the whole wide world. They're only one of two native Hawaiian mammals. The other is a bat (and if I'm gonna wanna save an animal, well, it's hard to pick a bat). Now, back to: ACTION!!

SCENE 7: SOS (SAVE OUR SEALS)

EXT. LANIKAI BEACH—10 MINUTES LATER

CAMERA WIDE SHOT of all the kids jumping out of the battered van. They race down a narrow path through bamboo hedges and come out onto a wide beach. Lulu leads the Ohana kids' stampede. Her hair flaps under her ALOHA cap. Uncle Akamu, even though he's a grandpa, sprints way ahead. He hauls plastic poles and netting, and wears an orange vest that says "Hawaiian Monk Seal Response Team O'ahu" on the back.

Uncle Akamu stops a hundred feet away from a black, furry BODY about four feet long. It doesn't move. Uncle Akamu puts up his large, browned hands. The kids slow and approach carefully. He puts his left forefinger to his lips and everyone becomes quiet.

LULU

(whispering to Noelani)

Seeing a monk seal is like one of my Hawaii dreams
come true.

Silently, Uncle Akamu and the children stake poles and attach netting. When they finish, they all sit and watch the black, fuzzy seal pup sleep.

UNCLE AKAMU
(speaking soft and low)
Keiki, mahalo. We put up this temporary pen to let this baby rest so nothing disturbs him.

LULU
Or her.

UNCLE AKAMU
Right. I'm not sure yet.

Maleko flops down on his back.

MALEKO
Hey, I can totally see how this guy could snooze here all day. This sand feels like a hundred pillows.

UNCLE AKAMU
Baby seals are born on soft sand. When they are big and strong enough, their mamas teach them to swim.

LULU
And till then, doesn't she have to feed her baby?

UNCLE AKAMU
(stares out to sea and his eyes rest on the postcard-perfect Mokulua Islands off shore)
Yes.

Noelani pulls up her legs under her chin. She closes her eyes and buries her face in her knees.

UNCLE AKAMU
(turns from the sea to look at Lulu)
Their mamas nurse them for about six weeks.
(looks around to all the kids)
Keiki, I don't know exactly how old this one is. But young.
Not more than fifty pounds. They're not usually without
their mamas till they're about two hundred pounds—

Lulu forgets about being still and quiet. She pushes herself up
off the sand and looks around.

LULU
(sounding frantic)
Then where's its mother? We haven't seen her.

Other kids now get to their feet and start scanning the beach
and ocean.

Uncle Akamu remains sitting.

UNCLE AKAMU
(voice stern but so quiet it can barely be heard over the
swooshing waves)
Sit.

All the children do as they are told, very quickly.

UNCLE AKAMU
(his eyes stare into the eyes of each child for a moment)
Lulu is right to worry that something happened to

this baby's mama. It is our *kuleana* now. Our job. Our responsibility is to protect this little one.

Warm, sweet chanting and a steady drumbeat drift toward the kids, the baby seal, and then out over the ocean.

All turn around to see Auntie Moana and Caridyn coming toward them. Dozens of VOLUNTEERS in orange vests follow behind them. They carry a stretcher, blankets, and bottles of milk. A stethoscope swings from one woman's neck.

SCENE 8: HULA ON HOLD

EXT. MOKULUA DRIVE—ONE HOUR LATER

The Ohana campers sit on the front lawn of the house where Uncle Akamu's van remains parked in a friend's driveway. They eat a late lunch.

LULU
(in between bites of sandwich)

You're not hungry, Noe? (swallows) How about a sip of my pineapple soda?

Lulu holds out a glass bottle to her friend. Noelani shakes her head.

LULU

Are you worrying about the baby seal's mother?

Noelani stares down at her ankles.

NOELANI

I'm worrying about my mom.

Lulu puts down her sandwich and soda, and studies her friend. She's never heard her talk about her mom before.

NOELANI
(continues in a super soft voice)
My mom's a Marine. She's off at sea, and I never know where exactly. I worry all the time she's not coming back and then I'll be just like that little fuzzy seal, alone on the beach.

Lulu reaches to hug her friend when...

BEEP, BEEP. A car horn blares on the quiet street. WIDE CAMERA SHOT as the car passes neat houses and gardens and heads closer.

Lulu looks up to see Khloe, Carole, and Cate sitting in a red convertible.

The car slows and then stops. Lulu gets up and stumbles over the curb.

LULU
(speaks super fast)
Aloha! Hey, we just helped save a baby monk seal! And, turns out, she's a girl! We're not sure where her mother is. Uncle Akamu is gonna sit on the beach all night to see if her mother comes back and if—

KHLOE

Well, here's *my* mom. Mom, this is Lulu...

(speaking her last name extra loud)

...HARRISON.

MRS. LYONS

(bubbly and excited)

Hiya, Lulu. I know all about your parents making a movie on the island. I really should meet them! I grew up right here on O'ahu, and I know everyone. I'm sure I can be helpful.

LULU

(to Mrs. Lyons)

Aloha, Mrs. Lyons.

Mrs. Lyons picks up her iPhone.

MRS. LYONS

(to Lulu)

Excuse me, sweetie. Have to answer a text. Someone's always looking for me.

Her pink nails clack on the screen.

KHLOE

So, are your mom and dad really going to be at the hula-off tomorrow?

CATE

'Cause we know making a movie is lots cooler than
watching Ohana Camp try and hula.

(giggles nervously)

Khloe notices Noelani sitting on the curb.

KHLOE

(calls to Noelani)

NOE!

Noelani gets up and stands next to Lulu.

KHLOE

Are you gonna dance tomorrow?

Noelani stares down at her toes. Lulu rushes into the awkward silence.

LULU

I'm excited that my parents are going to be at the hula-off
to meet my Ohana friends.

CAROLE

We'll believe it when we see it.

Lulu leans on the convertible.

LULU

(friendly)

It's too bad you're not on our team anymore.

Mrs. Lyons puts her phone away.

46

KHLOE

Mom! C'mon! We gotta get home and try on our costumes!

Khloe gives the puffy garment bag laying across her lap a little shake.

NOELANI

You have costumes?

CAROLE

Don't you?

LULU

(voice low, like she's sharing something)
We have a secret weapon.

Noelani gives Lulu the "what are you talking about" look. Lulu just winks back.

LULU

(turning back to Khloe and the Cs)
See ya tomorrow. But...
(pauses for dramatic effect)
...beware of our secret weapon! It's super-looper incredible.

Mrs. Lyons wiggles her long, pink-polished fingernails as the red convertible drives off.

NOELANI

(to Lulu)
But we don't have a secret weapon.

LULU

Sure we do! It's you! You're the best hula dancer on the island.

Noelani studies her toes more closely than ever.

 CUT!! Do you ever have one of those roller-coaster days? The kind that goes up really high and then races you back down? Then zooms you up and down a few more times? Well, that's this day. First, I was so excited to see that baby monk seal that I ran on muscles I didn't know I had. But when I started thinking something happened to her mother, I panicked. When the rescuers arrived, I got excited again. Learning about Noelani's mom, I felt myself starting to worry again. I have been so caught up in everything, I forgot about tomorrow's hula-off! So, instead of letting that roller coaster zip me down, I've got to get to work on Operation Secret Weapon and Operation Beg My Parents. OK, now that you understand what a roller-coaster day can be like, I better get back to the script. I've got a busy night ahead: ACTION!!

SCENE 9: DINNER WITH DESTINY

INT. ALAN WONG'S RESTAURANT, KING STREET— THURSDAY, 7 P.M.

Elevator opens to the third floor. Lulu bursts out. Alexis lingers in the elevator, giving Lulu a good head start.

Lulu still wears the sandy, damp, fishy-smelly clothes from her day at Ohana Camp—a SURF KAUAI T-shirt, orange skirt, and grungy, checkered Vans with the white squares colored in orange. At least Alexis got her to peel off her SPF 50 pants and shirt. Alexis wears a cropped, white, flowing cami with a semi-sheer mint maxi skirt and Stella McCartney thick-strapped sandals with a metal heel. She carries a nude tote, and her hair is twisted up in a tight bun.

Alexis feels pretty sure that if anyone she knows happens to see her with Lulu in this hyper-fancy, mega-cool casual restaurant, they'd never know she and Lulu are related.

The girls stop when they see the hostess. Lulu pulls off her ALOHA cap for the first time in hours. Her hair is completely flat on top and raging wild from her ears down.

ALEXIS
(in her most commanding L.A. teen girl voice)
Excuse me. We're here to have dinner with Mr. and Mrs. Harrison.

HOSTESS
Sure. They're out on the terrace. Follow me.

They enter the dimly lit restaurant. Alexis slyly checks out the other diners. Lulu wanders behind, checking out wood panels along the walls.

LULU
(to the hostess and pointing to the wall)
Pardon me, are those koa wood?

HOSTESS

Yes, they are.

Lulu squeezes between chairs. She reaches out to touch the wood-paneled wall and bumps, bangs, and brushes the back and hair of a distinguished Japanese gentleman.

LULU
(calls out)
Lex! Koa trees in Hawaii are like the Truffula trees in *The Lorax*. Remember that Dr. Seuss book? All the beautiful Truffula trees get chopped down.

ALEXIS
I skipped picture books and went straight for *Teen Vogue*. Which explains why you look like you stepped out of the pages of a Dr. Seuss book and I look, well, *très* chic. Now c'mon.

Alexis reaches out to tug Lulu's wrist. Lulu pulls away and knocks a waiter as he places down a hot platter of steamy clams. It teeters on the edge of the table. Within seconds, it plops into the neatly dressed gentleman's lap.

Lulu reaches to pick up the plate from the floor and bangs over a jar of peanut butter that had been on the corner of the table. It nearly hits her head.

LULU

Geez peas!

HOSTESS
(gushes)
Oh! Mr. Sanyo, I am terribly...

Alexis yanks Lulu away and out toward the patio.

ALEXIS
(angry whisper)
K. That's kinda a mega disaster. That guy's the owner
and president of the studio that's making Mom and
Dad's movie!

LULU
(whispers back)
Yeah, but he doesn't know who we are!

They reach their parents' table in the far corner of the glassed-in
patio. Lulu stumbles into one of two empty chairs facing the
dining room. Her dad and mom sit Celebrity Style—their backs
to the other diners, so people don't recognize them and come
over, asking for autographs.

LULU
Aloha, Mom and Dad!

Fiona daintily sniffs.

LINC
(smile playing on his lips)
Someone smells fishy.

                    ALEXIS
We're late because Lulu had to be picked up all the way
at Lanikai beach.

Linc smacks his elbows on the table and leans forward.

                    LINC
Lu, you smell like some kinda sea creature.

                    LULU
It was because of the monk seal. Right when we were
gonna practice for the hula-off, we had to go save the
seal pup.
              (pauses to draw a breath)
So, can you come tomorrow? Remember? I asked you
before. My Ohana Camp's in the O'ahu Hula-off. It's at
twelve noon.

Fiona bends toward Lulu, looking her in the eyes. She's firm and
clearly used to being in control of a situation.

                    FIONA
First, tell us the big fish story.

                    ALEXIS
It's really boring. I've heard it ten times.

Lulu grabs an eggroll from the table and chomps off the end.
Steam floats out. Lulu's eyes water from the heat in her mouth.

Alexis shakes her long hair.

ALEXIS

Here's the hula story. Lulu's group has a little problem: there's NO way they can win the competition tomorrow because they aren't the best. They're more like the worst.

LULU

Well, maybe we could've been better if we'd practiced today, but we couldn't because this baby seal was stranded.

LINC
(reaches out for Lulu's arm)
Girl, sometimes you just gotta cancel rehearsal.

LULU

A veterinarian from Waikiki Aquarium came and gave her a bottle. She seemed like—

A BOY and his FATHER tap Linc on the shoulder. They wear matching Hawaiian shirts. Linc slowly twists around.

FATHER

Oh. Wow! You really are Linc Harrison. My son would really like you to sign a menu.

The pudgy boy of about twelve doesn't move. The father grabs the long paper menu from the boy and holds it out to Linc, who smiles and politely signs.

ALEXIS
(ignoring the father and son)

So, will you guys come? For Lulu it's a matter of life or humiliation.

LULU

That's not totally true. We're gonna have a secret weapon.

ALEXIS
(to Lulu)
Like what? A catapult to shoot coconuts at the competition?

FIONA
(playful but firm)
Look, you two. I've got a movie to try to get back on track.

LULU
(speaking extra fast)
I just thought you guys haven't ever been able to come to see me perform in anything, and since this is a family summer, I just thought...

FIONA
(now very serious tone)
And I thought I'd have an easy summer making an action movie about a brave naval captain who saves the world, and all I get are flat performances.
(glares at Linc)
With actors bickering every moment they get.

LINC
(rising anger)
You're pushing us actors too hard.

FIONA
Well, Sanyo Studios pushes me even harder! They refuse to give me enough money to even finish the movie.

The man from Lulu's earlier mishap approaches and stands behind Linc's left shoulder.

LINC
That's not the actors' fault. Sanyo could be the world's biggest penny-pinching, stingy studio chief. His studio should just shovel over a little more money to make a spectacular action movie!

LULU
(to the man)
Aloha, sir. Geez peas, I hope I didn't ruin your dinner. Do you want to meet my parents?

Fiona springs from her chair, but she's unable to talk.

Fiona and Linc look at each other. Their faces redden.

MR. SANYO
Oh, we all know each other already. I'm the penny-pinching cheapo. And I believe I am disturbing your dinner right now.

Mr. Sanyo begins to back away but nods toward Linc and Fiona.

MR. SANYO
Pardon me, I heard all the diners twittering about how

Linc and Fiona Harrison were here. I thought I would bring my regards.

FIONA

Of course, Mr. Sanyo. So brilliant to see you. How long are you in Honolulu?

MR. SANYO

I'm on my way back to Japan from L.A.

Mr. Sanyo turns and marches away.

FIONA

What was the line, Lex, you said a moment ago? Something like "this is a matter of life and humiliation"?

SCENE 10: MAYBE BUT MAYBE NOT

INT. LULU'S BEDROOM—LATER THAT NIGHT

Lulu's room has the same blond-wood floor and bright, creamy whiteness as the rest of the house. There's bleached-white furniture and white down bedding. The differences between her room and the rest of the house: every surface of furniture is cluttered with a collection of orangey-sunrise shells, Kelly-green sea glass, and milky-colored coral Lulu's found on beach walks.

Lulu pulls an iPhone out of her I USED TO BE A PLASTIC BOTTLE tote bag. She turns the phone on and flops onto her bed next to Watson. It takes her a while, but she pulls up the list of four numbers under "Favorites" and taps NOELANI NUI. While it rings, Lulu pushes Watson's mouth out of an empty plastic container of Spam sushi.

NOELANI

Lulu? Hey.

LULU

Noelani, can you talk? We've gotta discuss something kinda, ahhhh, important.

Lulu reaches for a butterfly-shaped *li hing mui* (salty plum) lollipop from under her bed. She unwraps it and lets Watson take the first lick.

NOELANI
(concerned)
Sure. I just have to speak quietly. Tutu is sleeping. That's what it's like living with a grandma.

Lulu and Watson share the butterfly lick for lick until he crunches off a wing.

LULU

Well, I could yell this whole conversation if I wanted to. My mom and dad aren't coming home for hours. After dinner with Lex and me, they headed to a party. That's what it's like living with my parents.

NOELANI
(super-quiet voice)
Lu, don't complain. At least you know they're coming home.

LULU
(quiet voice back)
I know. Sorry, Noe. I think you're...GROSS!! Geez peas!

Watson retches up tiny chunks of lollipop and flecks of Spam. He sniffs the hot, sour-smelling mound that slowly absorbs into Lulu's white, fluffy, puffy comforter.

NOELANI
(sounding confused)
Really? That's not too nice, Lu.

LULU
Sorry. I mean Watson. A tutti-frutti-flavored *li hing mui* lollipop on top of six pieces of Spam sushi didn't agree with his tummy. He just threw up on my bed.

NOELANI
(giggling)
Lulu, you're brave to let that pug on your bed.

LULU
Hey, that's what I'm calling about. YOU really are brave.

NOELANI
Not true.

LULU

And you're the best hula dancer at Ohana Camp and probably on the whole island of O'ahu.

SILENCE.

LULU
(rubbing Watson's belly)
And if you dance in front of all of the rest of us tomorrow, we'll be able to follow you.

Noelani still doesn't respond.

LULU
(continues)
We'd be, like, your backup dancers. Most people wouldn't even notice our mistakes because they'd be amazed at how flow-y and perfectly you hula.

NOELANI
(softly, almost a whisper)
I wish I could. It's just...something in me gets scared. I freeze up at the thought.

LULU
But you won't be up there alone! We'd all be there with you.

NOELANI
That doesn't really help. I'd be facing the audience. Front and center. Oh gosh! I can't imagine it.

                    LULU

Here's what you do: imagine something that makes you
feel...what's the brave word in Hawaiian?

                  NOELANI

Koa.

                    LULU

Yea. Think about something that makes you feel super-
double-looper *koa*. Even close your eyes and let the brave
thought inside you take over.

SILENCE.

Watson nibbles the sick-smelling barf.

                    LULU

Mega-hyper-enormous GROSS!

                  NOELANI

I'll think about dancing in front.

Lulu shoves Watson with her feet.

                    LULU
                  (excited)

Noe! You can totally do it. And it's the ONLY way we
won't be totally pathetic tomorrow.

                  NOELANI
                (whispering)

I know.

                      60

SCENE 11: SHAKE IT, DON'T FAKE IT

EXT. 'IOLANI PALACE, ON LARGE PALACE LAWN— SATURDAY MORNING

WIDE SHOT of hundreds of brightly dressed children standing around in clusters. There are so many kids it seems like every hula class, school, club, or camp sent a team to this year's hula-off.

ZOOM IN ON Ohana Camp kids sitting together on the ground in the shadows of the grand three-story 'Iolani Palace. Their faded OHANA CAMP flag, stuck into the ground near them, hangs down. There's not a puff of breeze in the hot, moist air. A big bowl of Lulu's homemade mango salsa and a tub of taro chips sit in the middle of straw beach mats. Auntie Moana walks around, making sure all the kids drink enough water. Caridyn sits with the kids and softly beats her *pahu* drum.

 CUT!! Just so you know, right now, I'm over the tippy-top stressed. I'm worried about Noelani being able to lead our hula AND about Lex getting my parents off the set and here to watch. When I get up onstage, I'm gonna be shaking like a ti leaf! I wonder if, like a hundred years ago, Hawaiian kids ever felt this scared performing for the Hawaiian royalty? Did you know that Hawaii is the only state in the United States that was once its own kingdom with its own king and queen and real royal palaces? That's where we are now—on the grounds of Hawaii's fanciest palace. Back to: ACTION!!

61

Lulu watches Noelani's foot shake up and down.

> LULU
> (to Noelani)

You OK?

> NOELANI

I'm super-whopper nervous.

> LULU

Yeah but what's that brave word again?

> NOELANI

Koa.

> LULU

Just focus on your inner *koa.*

Lulu feels a tap on her shoulder. She turns quickly, thinking it's her parents.

CLOSE-UP reveals Khloe and the Cs wearing matching aqua dresses.

They glance at Ohana kids chatting, giggling, eating, or just goofing around on the grass.

> KHLOE
> (to Lulu and Noelani)

How are my old partners from my Ohana Camp days? You guys danced yet?

LULU

Aloha, you guys. Nope, we haven't.

Carole gives Lulu a once-over.

CAROLE
(to Lulu)
So where're your famous parents?

CATE
I thought we'd get your dad's autograph?

KHLOE
I wish he was here to see our dance. We're gonna win.
We were perfect.
(glances at Cate and Carole)
Don't you guys think so?

CAROLE
Way for sure.

CATE
We danced *Ka wailele o Nu'uanu*. A song about a river
or something.

NOELANI
(softly, almost to herself)
It's about a waterfall.

CAROLE

Whatever. It's a hard hula, so just doing that dance is
gonna get us high points.

LULU
(looks at Noelani)

Do you know it?

Noelani nods.

Khloe and the Cs scamper off when they spot other girls wearing
the same aqua costume.

NOELANI
(to Lulu)

In case you were wondering, seeing them rained on my
teeny tiny *koa* flame.

Auntie Moana puts up her hand to stop Caridyn's drumming.

AUNTIE MOANA

Keiki, listen.

Ohana campers gather around.

AUNTIE MOANA

Uncle Akamu will not be coming to play ukulele for the
dance. He stayed up all night on the beach, waiting for
the little one's mother. At sunrise this morning, I got
him and put him to bed.

Some kids look down. Others twitch or wiggle. They do not want to be alarmed at performing without Uncle Akamu's ukulele because they know waiting and chanting for the seal pup's mother to come back is more important than hula. Still, they get nervous. No one looks at each other.

After a few quiet seconds, Lulu jumps up.

> LULU
>
> C'mon! I just heard them call Ohana Camp. Let's go.

Kids bolt up. Maleko and Liam sprint ahead.

Lulu scrambles after them. Her I USED TO BE A PLASTIC BOTTLE tote bag clonks her thigh as she runs.

> LULU
>
> Geez peas! Wait!

EXT. 'IOLANI PALACE GROUNDS, AREA BETWEEN STAGE AND JUDGE'S TABLE—CONTINUOUS

Auntie Moana *shhhs* all the kids. Lulu arrives. Between panting and pushing the stitch in her side, she reaches into her tote bag and pulls out yellow hibiscus and bobby pins.

> LULU
>
> I brought these for everyone. I almost forgot.

Lulu plunks down her tote bag and kids dive in for the flowers. Petals and fingers get crushed.

AUNTIE MOANA
Mahalo, Lulu. You brought the Hawaii state flower.

The girls pin them in their hair. The boys stick them onto their shirts.

LULU
I cut them from plants around my house this morning. You always say it's your favorite flower.

Lulu holds out a hibiscus to Auntie Moana. She leans down for Lulu to pin it in her hair, and while she does, Auntie's rough hand smooths Lulu's wild hair.

EXT. 'IOLANI PALACE, STAGE—CONTINUOUS

The cluster of Ohana Camp kids tries to make lines on the stage. Caridyn, her *pahu* drum pressed against her right hip, directs kids who scamper from one place to another. Lulu bumps into other campers. She's scanning the audience.

LULU
(stage whisper to Noelani)
I can't believe my mom and dad didn't come.

Noelani doesn't hear. She scoots into the back left corner leaving Lulu alone in front of the audience.

LULU
(loud)
Noelani! What are ya doing?

THWACK, TAP, THWACK, TAP. The drum begins. All the kids stand with their heels together but miss the starting cue. Caridyn bangs out the introduction again and again. Everyone stands motionless until the fourth time, when Kapono actually moves with a right tap.

> LULU
> (talks to herself out loud)
> One, two, three, tap. One, two, three, tap.

Without anyone to follow in front of her, Lulu goes left when she should go right and right when she should go left. Liam and Maleko burst into a spell of giggles, lose their place in the dance, and just shuffle from side to side. Not even Kenna and Kapono are coordinated with each other. Noelani performs with smooth swaying, perfect rhythm, and graceful arm motions, but with the clonking, bonking kids in front of and around her, no one sees her.

Every moment she can look up without falling on her face, Lulu scans the crowd.

THWACK, TAP. TAP, THWACK. The drum continues in perfect rhythm, even as the kids trip and bump into each other. And then...Lulu spots them!

CAMERA FOLLOWS—Fiona, in her high wedge shoes as she jogs toward the stage. She holds a black-and-white clapper. Linc, dark, aviator sunglasses; tousled, blond-streaked hair; baggy jeans; and a vintage, faded T-shirt that says "The ENGLISH BEAT" runs through the middle of the audience and onto the stage.

CAMERA ZOOMS ON ALEXIS, under a straw cowboy hat encircled by a leather-and-silver braided cord. She sits herself front and center, sets her iPhone to "Record," and points toward the stage.

Fiona now stands on the stage in front of Linc and the dancers. She snaps down the clapper.

FIONA
(loud, firm voice)
HILARIOUS HULA! Take One!

With a nod toward Caridyn, Fiona gets the music going again. This time, Linc Harrison performs the *hukilau* in the most exaggerated, hammed-up way ever seen on the grounds of the Royal Palace!

Linc sways his hips in a smooth rhythm. He's athletic and cool but performs playfully. His shoulders, arms, and hands bend and flow. A giant, handsome smile lights up his face below his sunglasses. Without missing a beat, he plucks the hibiscus from Lulu's hair and chomps it in his teeth, like a flamenco dancer. He sways his way to Maleko and Liam and knocks his hips in each of their directions so they bang into him. Linc spins over to the twins and twirls Kenna first and then Kapono.

The audience's laughing and clapping are so thunderous, coconuts in the nearby trees quiver.

Linc sashays over to Caridyn and square dances around her. There's no question why Linc Harrison is a movie star. The audience can't get enough of him. He thrives on the audience's cheers.

CAMERA CUTS TO ALEXIS. She's filming but catches Khloe and the Cs sitting stiffly behind her. While keeping her iPhone forward, Alexis glances over her shoulder and flashes them a smile and a thumbs-up.

ALEXIS
(under her breath)
Don't mess with a big girl, girls.

Caridyn bangs out a jazzy, swift, improvised tune to finish up. Linc puts his arm around Lulu's waist and does a little can-can.

The drumming stops and before the last THWACK floats away on the warm air, the audience goes wild. Fiona glides back to the center of the stage and smacks down the clapper.

FIONA
That's a print!

Ohana kids mob Linc. They whoop and high-five. Linc flashes them each a picture-perfect smile. He slaps the boys on the back and hugs the girls.

Lulu leaps from the stage and runs toward Alexis.

LULU
Lex! You got them here.

ALEXIS

An hour away from the set on a Saturday, no big deal. I knew I could pull it off.

LULU
(putting out her hand to high-five her sister)
Here's to Sister Power!

ALEXIS
(slapping Lulu's outstretched palm)
Here's to Payback.

INT. 'IOLANI PALACE, GRAND STAIRCASE—THIRTY MINUTES LATER

Knowing about a small side door, Liam and Maleko sneak the Ohana kids into the grand, four-story palace. Inside, it's quiet and cool. Fearing being caught, the kids scamper up the wide, wood staircase. At the top floor, they flop down, laughing and talking at once.

KENNA
Wow, Lulu! I'd never met a real actor before.

KAPONO
Neither have I.

The twins look at each other and crack up.

MALEKO
Guess who actually won the hula-off?

With his hands, Maleko drums a *ta-da* drum roll on the wood banister.

> ALL KIDS TOGETHER
> Island School of Hula.

All laugh.

> LIAM
> Who would want to be as boring as them?!

Noelani huddles by herself on a stair. She turns her body into a tight ball by hugging her legs to her chest. Lulu smooshes in next to her friend.

> LULU
> (to all the kids)
> I've found where all of Hawaii's koa trees went. (Waves her hands over the stairs.) Look at this staircase! How many do ya think they had to chop down to make this?

Liam gives a here-she-goes-again look to Maleko.

> LIAM
> We perform the greatest hula in history, and you want to talk about dead trees?!

> MALEKO
> Our *Hilarious Hula* already has more than five hundred YouTube hits. And it's only been up for, like, twenty minutes!

LULU

Well, my sister doesn't waste time getting anything out into the cyber world.

Ohana kids huddle around Maleko's iPhone screen and watch their now-famous performance. Noelani, however, remains on her stair, squeezing her knees and staring at her toes.

NOELANI
(softly to Lulu)
It's my fault.

LULU
(joking)
What's your fault? Chopping down a zillion endangered trees to build this grand staircase?

NOELANI

Everything. I told you I wasn't brave. I just couldn't dance up front.

LULU
(talking softly to her friend)
Don't worry about it, Noe. Geez peas! No one's bummed.
Ohana Camp put on a great hula show!

Noelani hides her face in her folded knees. Lulu rests her hand on her pal's shoulder.

Lulu watches Noelani's tears run down her leg. The drips slide from her eyes, stream down her face, over her knees, and continue slipping down to her ankles.

LULU
You're turning into a waterfall.

NOELANI
(into her knee caps)
My mom is so brave. She's a Marine, training people on an aircraft carrier. And me? Today I hid in back like a total chicken!

LULU
No one thinks that except you.

The Ohana kids wander around the palace. Lulu and Noelani listen to their friends chuckling and chatting as they explore.

LULU
I know you're really brave. It's just today wasn't your brave day.

Lulu reaches into her I USED TO BE A PLASTIC BOTTLE bag and yanks out a green, heart-shaped *li hing mui* lollipop. Lulu unwraps and starts licking.

                    NOELANI
    You're not supposed to eat in the palace.

Lulu offers Noelani a lick.

                    NOELANI
    Lulu, you're the Ohana Camp hero today. You saved us
    from total embarrassment and bitter defeat.

                    LULU
    Not me. It was my whole family. They came through
    because that's what families do—they support each other.

HAWAII FIVE-0 MUSIC RINGTONE comes from Lulu's bag. She reaches inside and withdraws an iPhone in a SAVE THE EARTH case.

                    LULU
                (into the phone)
    Hi, Lex. (pause) I thought you left with Mom and Dad?
    (pause) OK, I'm coming right now.

Lulu hangs up, then stares right into her friend's deep eyes.

                    LULU
                (speaks really fast)
    Noe, this is my best and first family summer ever. And

guess what? This summer you're gonna be a member of the Harrison Ohana.

NOELANI

What do you mean?

LULU

I'm going to figure out another chance for you to hula. That's what families do. Help each other.

NOELANI

I'm petrified even thinking about standing in front of people.

Lulu clomps down the grand koa wood staircase.

LULU

(voice echoes as she hollers up to Noelani)
That'll be our summer goal! Get you brave enough to hula and show this island who's really the best!

Lulu darts out the palace's side door.

 CUT!! Don't you think things happen in crazy ways? This hula-off is a perfect example of how life can be nutty, but good things happen if you pull together with your sister and BEG your parents to do something—like leave work to help you not die of embarrassment dancing hula. And, because I have this amazing family acting as, well, a family this summer, I'm sure they won't mind helping me get Noelani through her stage fright. As usual, I've got an idea but no plan, so I better get back to: ACTION!!

SCENE 12: QUIET ON THE SET

EXT. DIAMOND HEAD HAWAII FILM STUDIO—HALF HOUR LATER

Tall metal gates swing open. Maya drives a white Prius through the main studio entrance as a guard in the booth waves her through.

WIDE SHOT OF Maya's car as it slowly drives through the studio, past the makeup trailer and prop house. It pulls up next to Alexis's black Volkswagen Bug parked in front of a tiny house called a bungalow. Lulu leaps from the car. Alexis pauses and reapplies coral-colored lip shimmer and strokes a Mason Pearson brush through her long hair.

INT. PRODUCTION OFFICE BUNGALOW—CONTINUOUS

The small bungalow is filled with schedules, scripts, clipboards, and frantic PRODUCTION ASSISTANTS. Every type of power charger known to man or woman is plugged in around the small space. Smartphones, iPads, laptops, walkie-talkies, wireless headsets—any communication tool that needs power, there's a cord for it. MAXWELL, an eighteen-year-old guy with curly blond hair and khaki shorts, shouts his crisp British accent into a phone.

> MAXWELL
> Finish the auditions ASAP. Fiona wants all those extras on the set in two days!

Maxwell notices the sisters. He smiles and gives a thumbs-up to Lulu and a wink to Alexis.

Maxwell hangs up and turns his full attention to Alexis and Lulu.

                    MAXWELL
              (kind, warm voice)
Sorry. That was the casting director.

                     LULU
Aloha, Maxwell. Where're my parents? I gotta tell them how great it was that they came to my hula-off. They made it so fun, and my friends loved it.

                    ALEXIS
              (light, flirty, smiling)
But they went tearing out of the hula thing and stranded me there.

                    MAXWELL
And that would be because after Linc and Fiona went zipping off with you, Alexis, the head of the studio, Mr. Sanyo, happened to pop by and visit the set.

                     LULU
He DID??!

                    MAXWELL
He jolly did. He wanted to have a chat with the director about cutting costs on the movie.

ALEXIS

Fiona isn't good at doing anything on the cheap.

MAXWELL

Well, she better start, and while she's at it, she better hurry up and finish production.

LULU

I'm gonna see if there's anything I can do to help!

Lulu bolts out the door.

MAXWELL
(to Alexis)

As much as I'd love your beautiful company, I think you better grab your sister before she's found on the set. Unless, of course, you want to see Queen Fiona do that "off with her head" thing to your sister.

Alexis flips her silky hair in Maxwell's direction.

ALEXIS
(standing up)

If I didn't think my head would roll too, I'd hang out all day.

Alexis races out the door.

Maxwell calls after her.

MAXWELL

Hilarious Hula was smashing, Lex. If *Seas the Day* folds,
Linc and Fiona should switch from action films to comedy.

INT. DIAMOND HEAD STUDIO, MAIN SOUND STAGE— CONTINUOUS

The ginormous dark space is large enough to park a couple of 747
airplanes. It's cool inside, thanks to huge air conditioners blasting
freezing air.

Lulu bounds through darkness toward tall directors' chairs placed
behind a row of movie cameras on wheels. Every few feet she trips
on cords and cables. Then she bumps into the catering table.

CATERING ASSISTANT

Vegan or non?

LULU

What?

CATERING ASSISTANT

Are you vegan or non-vegan? We've got two different
catering areas depending on which way you eat. This is
the non-vegan table.

LULU

Mahalo for asking. I'm definitely non-vegan. But I'm just
looking for...

Alexis comes up behind Lulu and grabs her arm.

ALEXIS

(whispering)

Listen, if you want to see another sunset over the Pacific Ocean, I suggest we get out of here before anyone knows we're alive.

LULU

(soft, thoughtful tone)

Hey, Lex, I'm glad we're in this together.

Alexis releases Lulu's shoulder.

Alexis yanks a bunch of her silk-like hair, something she does when she's thinking.

ALEXIS

I'm trying to get us out of it together. We've got to lie low for a while and let Mom and Dad work.

LULU

(loud whispers)

But maybe we can help, just like Mom and Dad did for me and my friends.

ALEXIS

Look, I don't want to get in mega trouble or, worse, sent back to L.A. I've got more bikini shopping to do! And, Maxwell's really cu...

A tall, slim, but muscular man in a perfectly clean, pressed naval officer's uniform strides up to the girls. He shines a flashlight in their eyes.

NAVAL OFFICER
(deep voice)
Quiet on the set!

Alexis shakes with fright.

LULU
Yes, sir.
(then, focusing her eyes on the Officer)
DAAAAD?

Linc flashes a wide grin. He looks great in his costume. He gives them both sharp salutes.

ALEXIS
You look so totes cool!

LINC
Like a guy who's gonna save America?

Heels can be heard clicking closer.

LULU
Geez peas! You look like someone who could save the WHOLE world!

FIONA
(furious, frosty tone)
How about you start by saving this movie from being shut down?

LINC
(looking from Lulu to Alexis)
And that would be your mother.

Linc gives the girls a nervous "we're in for it now" smile.

LINC
Too bad we don't have the real United States military to
come save us right now.

Fiona points a long, thin finger at Linc.

FIONA
(stares coldly at him)
Where are you going in costume?

LINC
(grinning)
Just catching some bad guys who entered our territory
illegally.

Linc winks at Lulu.

FIONA
(icy, scary voice)
Alexis and Lulu. I don't know why you're on my set.
But since you are, I can tell you myself that summer
vacation is CANCELED. Dinners together are OFF.

ALEXIS
Got it, Fiona.

FIONA

Linc and I will now be working twenty-four/seven.

LULU

Mom, how about me and Lex and my friends help on the movie? We could carry stuff and be extras and anything you need to save some money and—

Fiona spins around to examine Lulu. Her ALOHA cap is smashed over her hair. Her battered tote bag is slung over her mango-stained SURF KAUAI T-shirt, and her white SPF undergarments shine in the dark. She hardly looks like someone who'd work on a movie, unless, of course, she were the actress dressed in costume to play an eleven-year-old character who survived a shipwreck and floated to Hawaii on a rubber raft.

FIONA

Look, my focus has bounced around all summer, and now I've got this movie hanging from a string.
(pause while she mindlessly tugs at her gold watch)
I could run out of money before I can shoot the final big military landing.

LULU

Mom, it's my fault.

FIONA

(voice softens)
Lulu, darling, what are you even talking about?

Alexis jumps in.

                    ALEXIS
It's my fault too.

Fiona looks from Alexis to Lulu while she clicks her clean, perfect nails polished in OPI's gel color called Samoan Sand.

                    FIONA
It's all our faults.

Fiona gives each girl a quick hug.

                    FIONA
Now understand.
                    (pauses)
This...
                (waves her hands around)
...is a movie. A job. A business. It is NOT summer vacation.

Fiona strides back toward her director's chair and the five people hovering around it waiting to ask her questions.

                    FIONA
        (without turning around or slowing her walk)
    And, Lincoln Harrison, BACK TO WORK!

 CUT!! I can't let this moment pass without telling you that right now, everything I've eaten all day is gushing and sloshing around. My belly feels like a washing machine on the fastest spin cycle. My perfect family summer just ended. Except, I can't stop wondering if there's anything I can do. There's got to be plenty of work to do for the movie. And a family supports each other—through thick and thin. OK, back to: ACTION!!

ACT II: BIG LIFE ON A SMALL ISLAND

SCENE 1: PUG IN THE BUG

INT. ALEXIS'S VOLKSWAGEN BUG—THURSDAY AFTERNOON

Lulu is squished into the backseat of Alexis's beloved car. Watson's head hangs out the window, and Lulu holds tightly to his leash.

Even though Alexis goes to the beach every day, there's not a spec of sand in her car. And even though Alexis doesn't surf, there's a surfboard rack on the car's roof.

Lulu munches taro chips from a cut-down pillowcase. Alexis sings along with Katy Perry playing off her iPhone through her car speakers.

> ALEXIS
> (glances at Lulu in the rearview mirror)
> I better not find a greasy shred of chip in my car.

Lulu grabs out a handful of oily chips and reaches toward Alexis.

LULU
(mouth munching)
Wanna try my homemade taro chips? They taste a lot like corn chips.

Alexis turns down the music.

ALEXIS
Maybe you didn't hear *moi*? I don't want you eating it in my car!

LULU
Geez peas, Lex. This isn't supposed to be a car ride anyway. It's Watson's walk!

Lulu catches Alexis's eye in the rearview mirror and they both laugh.

ALEXIS
OK. I've got to admit, Lu. Great idea. Walking Watson L.A. style works *très* fab in Hawaii.

CAMERA SHOT FROM ABOVE THE CAR. Shows the black Bug speeding along a beach road with the pug hanging halfway out the left rear window. His ears flap in the wind.

LULU
And, ummm, I have another good idea.

ALEXIS

One a summer is enough.

LULU

This has to do with Mom and Dad!

ALEXIS

Whatever it is, it's a NO.

Alexis swerves too fast and Watson flies into the car. He slowly unrolls himself from a ball and starts licking chip crumbs that have fallen on the seat.

LULU

This summer was supposed to be about our family spending time together. And, ya know, lots of kids help their parents work, especially in the summer. Let's come up with something we can do.

ALEXIS

And lots of girls, like *moi*, build up their bikini collection over the summer. That's what I plan to do.

LULU

How many bathing suits do you need 'cause didn't you just buy—

Alexis cranks up her music. The last thing she wants to discuss with Lulu is how her newest pair of red, ruffled bikini bottoms sag.

Lulu taps Alexis on her bony right shoulder. Alexis turns and flashes Lulu a "this must be an emergency" look over her shoulder.

LULU
You better pull over. Watson has to poop.

Watson squats in the corner of the backseat. Tootsie Roll shaped poops hit Alexis's white upholstery at the same time she screams over her loud music.

Alexis glowers at Watson through her rearview mirror.

ALEXIS
Lu! You and that nutty dog are back to actually WALKING on your walks! And NO more of your crazy schemes.

SCENE 2: NOT BLOWING OVER

EXT. LEDGE OVERLOOKING THE HALONA BLOWHOLE—MONDAY MORNING

Lulu, Noelani, and the Ohana Camp kids wander the windy ledge above a large rock formation. They stare out toward the ocean, waiting for the next spray to rise into the air.

KAPONO
(scary voice right into his twin's ear)
There's a monster under there!

KENNA
(her soft voice quivers)

Really?

LULU

No, he's kidding!

KAPONO

The spiky evil creature used to breathe out fire, but so much water got into his mouth, now he can only breathe out boiling mist.

KENNA
(frightened)

Can the monster still move?

LULU

There's no monster.
(to Noelani)

Talk about being scared, I think Lex and I almost ruined our parents' movie.

NOELANI

Wait. You did?

LULU

The head of the studio that paid kazillions of dollars to make *Seas the Day* came to Mom's set, and she wasn't there.

NOELANI
(softly)
That's not 'cause of you. Where was she?

Suddenly, Lulu's mouth seems dry. Her lips feel stuck together.

LULU
At the hula-off.

Awkward silence.

NOELANI
Oh no.

LULU
Oh yes.

NOELANI
(small, scared voice)
That's 'cause of me.

LULU
Not at ALL. Geez peas. My mom explained that she and Dad coming to the hula-off didn't cause their movie to be in trouble. But I'm not sure...

NOELANI
(even smaller, quieter voice than before)
I don't know anything about making movies, so I don't know either.

91

LULU

I'm trying to figure out some way to help my mom and dad, just like they helped Ohana Camp.

NOELANI

Good idea. Like what?

Luckily, the monster saves Lulu from answering.

Little Kenna tugs the bottom of Lulu's orange skirt. Lulu picks her up.

LULU
(to Kenna)
It's not a monster at all. It's just nature. Don't worry! Thousands of years ago, boiling, bubbling lava from an erupting volcano created this hollow tube. Down there...
(points to the ocean)
...here's what's happening right now. Wave water is filling up the lava tube and pushing down and down where the tube is smaller and smaller. Any moment, the pressure will force a stream of water to shoot up.

PHFFFFFUUUUUUU!!! The water sprays up almost thirty feet in the air.

The Ohana kids and other visitors gasp and snap pictures.

KENNA
(who had been looking at Lulu)
I missed it!

Lulu puts Kenna down. She pulls out her iPhone.

                    LULU
            (to Noelani and Kenna)
I'm gonna film the next blow. That way, we can watch the
water blast whenever we want. And I'll send Hawaiian
nature to my BFF Sophia in L.A. She'll love it too.

As the girls wait for the next aquatic explosion, Lulu, phone
switched to filming mode, focuses on the spot where the blowhole opens.

PHFFFFFUUUUUU!!! The water shoots toward the sky.

                    LULU
Got it!

The kids gather around and watch it on the small iPhone screen.

                    LULU
            (to the group around her)
OK, gotta admit, the last thing I ever wanted was this
complicated phone, but it's cool to make a mini-movie.

                    LIAM
Like *Hilarious Hula*. Thousands of people keep
watching it!

                    MALEKO
Lulu, you've gotta get your parents to make another
video with us.

> LULU
> (sadly)

Not this summer.

> (pause)

Maybe not even in this lifetime.

Noelani tugs Lulu to a nearby rock. Lulu plunks down.

> NOELANI

That was really sweet how you made Kenna feel brave.
> (looks under the ALOHA hat brim into Lulu's eyes)

Lu, you're good at doing everything. I'm sure you'll figure
out something to help your parents, and we'll all help.
> (looks toward the Ohana kids)

> LULU

The problem is I really don't know anything about
making movies either.

> NOELANI

Just help with something you like to do.

A deep, long honking sound gives Lulu a moment to think.

> NOELANI

Uncle Akamu's blowing the conch. It's time for lunch.

Lulu stays seated on the rock.

> NOELANI

C'mon. Aren't you hungry?

Noelani takes Lulu's hands and, with effort, hauls her up.

LULU

That's it! Lunch! There's this fancy caterer who sets up food on the set every day. I bet I could make lunch for the crew, like on weekends, and save the movie money.

NOELANI

That's a lot of food to cook by yourself—

LULU

I can ask Maya to help me.

NOELANI

We'll all cook with you.

LULU

MAHALO! Awesome. Let's tell everyone! My house! This weekend.

Lulu dashes toward the others while pushing her ALOHA hat more firmly onto her head to keep it from blowing off.

SCENE 3: TAKE IT TO THE TOP

EXT. KAHALA RESORT, VALET ENTRANCE—FRIDAY EVENING

CAMERA FOLLOWS Alexis's black Bug speeding up a long black driveway. The car screeches to stop at a waiting valet.

Alexis takes a moment to spray her Jo Malone French Lime Blossom perfume before slowly stepping from her car.

LULU
(calls out from the backseat)
Hey, Lex. I don't know why you're spraying perfume. The real plumeria flowers around this driveway smell better than your perfume.

ALEXIS
Just stay in the car while I dash in and bring Mom her gold clutch.

LULU
I wanna come. I've got to talk to Mom and Dad.

Lulu scrambles out of the car. Her SURF OAHU T-shirt hangs below her skirt. Her brown messy hair flies around her face while the top of her hair is mushed under her ALOHA cap.

ALEXIS
(annoyed voice)
Look, Lu. Mom and Dad changed at the studio to get to this *très* glam party on time. It's like the governor of Hawaii is supposed to be here or something. Mom forgot this purse. She's in mega-stress mode. Stay away!

Lulu plops into a white cushiony chair while fancy cars drive up to the valet and fancy-dressed guests get out one after another. Lulu closes her eyes and breathes in the flowery-smelling air. After a moment, she feels a tug on her right arm.

CARIDYN

Lulu?

UNCLE AKAMU
(smiling)
Did you run away from home?

Uncle Akamu wears a ti leaf skirt over his shorts. Caridyn wears a traditional muumuu.

LULU

Hey! You guys look great.

CARIDYN

You OK? We're late for our show.

UNCLE AKAMU

Want to watch? I'm performing the fire dance. Big private luau here tonight for the governor of Hawaii and—

Lulu springs to her feet.

LULU

Geez peas! My parents are going to be at your luau. I need to talk to them anyway.

Uncle Akamu and Caridyn look at each other but don't have time to discuss Lulu. They walk through the high-ceiling lobby. Lulu bounces behind them. They get outside, pass a large, manmade lagoon, and head toward the beach, where burning torches are stuck into the sand.

Before they reach the hum of voices and soft music of the party, there's a SPLASH!

LULU
(hollers)

What was that?!

Lulu twirls around and starts running toward the sound of wet splatter.

SPLASH and SPRAY!

LULU
(shouting)

Dolphins?!

Within moments, there's another splash, but this time Lulu hears it from underwater. In the darkness, she's run into the lagoon.

CAMERA UNDERWATER. Four sleek gray dolphins zoom past Lulu's fingertips. Their bodies gleam silvery in the moonlight.

Lulu waves at the dolphins every time they glide near her. Within moments, though, she is pulled up.

UNCLE AKAMU
(swimming with Lulu tucked under his arm)

OK?

LULU
(head skimming above the surface)
I'm fine!

EXT. KAHALA HOTEL—VALET ENTRANCE, TWENTY MINUTES LATER

Lulu sits wrapped in luxurious, thick hotel towels. A frothy coconut shake and wedge of pineapple cake sit on a little table next to her.

LULU
(to hotel bellman who offers her a blanket)
Mahalo. But, really, I'm fine.

CLICK CLACK CLICK CLACK is heard getting closer and closer.

ALEXIS
(from across the lobby)
You are SO not fine!

Fiona, in a shimmering gold gown, and Linc, in a slim-cut tailored suit, race over to Lulu and hug her through her mummy-wrapped towels.

LINC
(lightheartedly)
What are you doing swimming with the fish?

FIONA
(stern voice)
What are you doing at this hotel?

ALEXIS
What are you doing out of my car?

Alexis stares hard at Lulu. Her violet eyes drill into Lulu.

LULU
(speaking super-dooper fast)
Mom and Dad, I can be useful on *Seas the Day*. I want to
help with the food. I'm a really good coo—

FIONA
(while quickly reapplying her Chanel lipstick)
Lu, seriously, this isn't the time or place.

Another hotel bellman approaches. He hands Lulu her
soggy ALOHA cap.

LULU
Geez peas, what a nice hotel. They even fished my hat
out of the water.

LINC
(smiling)
Before the dolphins ate it.

There's a swirl of activity as a long, white car pulls up. The tall,
elegant Mr. Sanyo steps out. He wears a pressed, soft-gray suit
and green Hermès tie. His hair is perfectly trimmed above his
ears. His fingernails are clean and buffed to a perfect shine.

FIONA
(under her breath to Linc)
There's Sanyo.

LINC
He's arriving WITH the governor?

FIONA
(to Lulu and Alexis)
Now get home, please.

LULU
Wait!
(jumps up and her towels fall to the floor)
I came to ask if I can bring lunch for you guys and the whole crew? OK? This Sunday? We're gonna cook a traditional Hawaiian me—

Linc strides toward the approaching Mr. Sanyo and claps him on the shoulder.

FIONA
(sharp whisper)
Fine, Lulu. Just get out of here!

She gracefully glides over to Linc, Mr. Sanyo, and the governor of the great state of Hawaii.

 CUT!! I've got to admit that sometimes getting your parents' attention is harder than other times. I didn't mean to take a dip with the dolphins to get them out of their party. Actually, I wouldn't have minded sneaking into the fancy luau and watching Caridyn and Uncle Akamu perform. But, from one kid to another: when the opportunity to swim with dolphins comes up, take it no matter what—even with your clothes on. Now back to: ACTION!!

SCENE 4: GETTING FRESH

EXT. KAPI'OLANI COMMUNITY COLLEGE FARMERS' MARKET—SATURDAY, 7:30 A.M.

Lulu and Maya scurry through O'ahu's biggest farmers' market where everything is Hawaiian grown or made.

CAMERA FOLLOWS Lulu and Maya. They take turns pushing what looks like an airport baggage cart. They pass bananas, pineapples, mangos, coconuts, macadamia nuts, and supersized dinosaur kale.

Lulu heads left. Maya yanks her right.

> LULU
> (shaking her moppy hair)
> I know this shortcut to get to the Paniolo Kettle Korn.

> MAYA
> Good, except kettle corn's not on the *Seas the Day* luncheon menu. This way.

Lulu follows but soon wanders toward a baked goods stall. She sniffs baskets of freshly baked taro sweet bread. Maya tugs her along.

MAYA
Do you know how long it takes to cook *laulau*? C'mon.

They turn down an aisle that feels like a tropical forest. There are all sizes and colors of orchid plants. Lulu pauses to stroke a waxy, shiny red anthurium and pricks her finger on a tiny green pineapple growing on a miniature tree.

MAYA
(calling out)
Move it, Lu. We gotta cook Hawaiian plate lunch for seventy people and deliver it by noon!

Lulu and Maya stop at a seafood vendor. Lulu stares deeply into the eyes of formerly alive *opah* (moonfish). Maya buys twenty-five pounds of butterfish.

They load up their cart with pork, chicken, mangos, and sacks of chocolate-covered macadamia nuts.

On the way to the car, they roll past the prepared-food stalls. Lulu deeply breathes in and out through her nose so many times she's about to be dizzy.

LULU
(to Maya)
If I could invent my own perfume, it would be the smell

of steaming, roasting, frying, scrambling, barbecuing, baking, and sizzling that I smell right now.

Maya's dark, soft almond-shaped eyes fold in the corners as she smiles.

                    MAYA
Truthfully, Lulu, making perfume from the scent of cooking food might be easier than cooking lunch for your parents' movie crew.

SCENE 5: COOKING UP A STORM

INT. HARRISONS' KITCHEN—SUNDAY, 11:30 A.M.

Lulu, her hair bunched and scrunched under her ALOHA hat, sits on a stool trying to wrap little balls of chopped, seasoned fish and pork into taro leaves. The meaty, fishy balls keep splatting onto the floor.

Watson circles under Lulu. Every time a morsel hits the blondwood floor, Watson licks it up and then rubs his bulging stomach over the wet spot left by his tongue.

Noelani perches next to Lulu. She wraps the pork and fish filling like a pro. Liam stands next to Noelani and ties big ti leaves around each of her neat green balls.

LIAM
Lulu, you better hurry 'cause I don't think I've tied up more than two of your *laulau*. The ones I'm doing are all Noelani's.

LULU
The fish and pork pieces don't stay inside my leaves. Making *laulau* is harder than I thought.

NOELANI
Cooking for so many people is harder than I thought.

Maya slides six *laulau* into the steamer.

MAYA
We better get more *laulau* packets dropped in the steamer oven soon or we'll end up bringing them raw!

Noelani reaches over and helps Lulu.

Auntie Moana and Uncle Akamu enter. Their wise eyes sweep around the room. The Harrisons' usually spotless kitchen is spotted beyond recognition. Pots, pans, bowls, spoons, knives, cutting boards, and electric choppers, mixers, and blenders cover every surface from the countertop to the stovetop. Water puddles under Kenna and Kapono, who just got out of the pool but are now slicing mangos for salsa. Children's chatter mixes with the sound of the waves crashing outside the open kitchen windows. The loudest noise, however, is Maleko, who bangs, taps, and clangs spoons between stirring the macaroni and rice.

Lulu waves.

LULU

Aloha! We had a late start. Before we got cooking, I taught everyone how to make my special coconut shake.

AUNTIE MOANA

In fifteen minutes, we're supposed to drive all the food over to the studio. What's done?

Lulu stands up and knocks a mound of ti leaves to the floor.

LULU

Geez peas! I don't think anything is actually ALL done.

Maya looks up from the steamer oven as she pulls out *laulau*.

MAYA

Moana, Akamu, pick up a spoon or something. We need your hands because—

KENNA
(cries out)
AHHHH! I'm gushing blood!

Everyone rushes to where Kenna holds her little bloody finger over mushy, mangled pieces of mango.

KAPONO
(guilty voice)
I didn't push your hand. You cut yourself all by yourself!

KENNA
(through tears)
You did too.

(looks at Lulu)
I might have gotten squirts of my blood in your famous mango salsa.

LULU
Probably will taste fine. I can add it as one of my ingredients.

Auntie Moana takes Kenna by the hand that doesn't have a bleeding finger.

AUNTIE MOANA
Come. Let's clean you up.

MAYA
(to Lulu)
That's now four hands gone.

Lulu looks at the Ohana kids all now standing around where Kenna had been seated.

LULU
(panicky)
You guys, we've gotta get these lunches to Diamond Head Studio or else I'm...well...toast!

SCENE 6: SICK ON THE SET

INT. DIAMOND HEAD STUDIO, BACK OF SOUND STAGE—12:30 P.M.

MAXWELL
(joking to Lulu)
It doesn't look like your food has killed anyone yet.

Maxwell flashes Lulu a playful smile. He runs his fingers through his bushy hair while Alexis grins at him. Alexis gracefully sits down on a folding chair next to him.

LULU
People don't die from delicious, home-cooked food.

A tall, paper-thin actress with white-blond hair approaches.

ACTRESS
(looks from Alexis to Lulu)
Which of you is the daughter who's the cook? How divine that Linc and Fiona have their own chef?!

Two men who work on the set sit down with plates of *laulau*, macaroni salad, and rice. Maxwell introduces them as the KEY GRIP and SOUND ENGINEER.

SOUND ENGINEER
(with mouth full)
Delicious lunch.

LULU

Mahalo. Glad you like the plate lunch.

Linc drapes an arm around Lulu's shoulder.

LINC
(teasing)
This is my daughter who could be a professor or a chef or in trouble for something or another.

LULU

Daaad!

LIAM
(shouts through the open stage door)
C'mon, Lulu! We're going!

Lulu looks outside. The Ohana kids wave their arms from the parking lot. They have just returned from a tour around the studio with Fiona.

Lulu stands. Pauses at Alexis.

LULU
(to Alexis)
Can you bring me home?

ALEXIS
(flashes her big violet eyes at Lulu)
Not a chance.

MAXWELL

She's gonna stay for a while. I'll keep her busy.

Lulu rolls her eyes and heads across the sound stage to join her friends when SUDDENLY—

ACTRESS

Call an ambulance!!

The Actress clutches her stomach and doubles over in pain. Linc rushes to her side. Alexis, always fast with her phone, punches in 911.

Key Grip stands but then slumps back down. His crew of grips, brawny guys who do the hauling, hanging, and repairing on the set, kneel over their boss.

KEY GRIP
(mumbling)

I'm so dizzy. I can't stand.

MAXWELL
(in a raspy voice)

My insides are squirming like venomous snakes.

Fiona staggers in from the parking lot. The Sound Engineer races to help her.

FIONA

I'm not sure if I'm seasick from filming boat scenes or if I'm going to die.

SOUND ENGINEER
(to Fiona)

Sorry, darling.

Sound Engineer lets go of Fiona, who crumples to the ground. The Sound Engineer retches a few feet away.

Linc crawls over to Fiona but stops every few inches to squeeze his arms across his stomach as if he's holding his guts in place.

LULU
(frantic)
Mom! Dad! Are you going to live?!

ALEXIS
(tossing her long, skinny arm around Lulu's neck)
They'll probably live but then they'll kill you.

MOANING and GAGGING echo around the vast sound stage. SCREAMS of sirens become louder and louder.

SCENE 7: PICKING UP

INT. NOELANI'S SIMPLE, SQUARE-SHAPED ONE-STORY HOUSE—LIVING ROOM MONDAY AFTERNOON

Framed pictures of a young, uniformed woman are propped up around the room. A faded green couch and wood coffee table fill the small, bright room. Half-filled plastic bins sit along a sun-splashed wall.

Lulu sprawls on the couch while Noelani stands in the middle of the living room. They play a game of charades with Hawaiian words. Noelani taps her heart and airily raises her hands towards the sky.

LULU

Birds?

Noelani shakes her head. She repeats her motions slowly and gracefully.

LULU

Heart attack?

Noelani shakes head again.

NOELANI

You're just totally guessing.

LULU

That's because I don't know at all.

Both girls GIGGLE. They don't notice Noelani's grandmother, TUTU, enter. She's carrying armfuls of old clothes.

TUTU

What was the word?

NOELANI

Akua.

(stares at Lulu)

It means "spirit."

TUTU

Well, that's a hard one.

Lulu springs from the couch. She takes the heavy pile of clothes from Tutu.

TUTU

Mahalo, Lulu. I was hunting for Noelani's baby clothes and found old uniforms belonging to Noelani's mom.

She holds up a blue coat.

LULU

(touches the coat)

Geez peas! It's heavy.

NOELANI

(small voice)

That's a dress uniform jacket.

TUTU

This isn't just any dress uniform jacket. This is the jacket your mom wore when she received her first medal.

LULU

She has more than one?!

TUTU

My daughter, Lieutenant Colonel Nui, has eight medals
so far.

LULU

(to Noelani)

Your mom's a real hero! My dad just plays one in the
movies!

NOELANI

My mom's really good at vanishing.

SILENCE.

Noelani scrunches into a ball on the floor. Lulu sits down near
her friend

LULU

There's no one who'd like to disappear more right now
than me. Maybe you can get me into the Marines?

Noelani smiles.

Tutu sits behind the girls on the couch and rests a hand on each
of their heads.

TUTU

So, Lulu, you learned yesterday that when you make
laulau, you have to keep the ti leaves and the taro leaves
separate. Ti leaf makes you sick if you eat it.

LULU
I also learned that my parents want to launch me into the ocean in an outrigger canoe without a paddle.

Tutu laughs.

TUTU
Actually, I talked to your mother a little while ago. She wants you to know that everyone's fine.

LULU
No one's in the hospital?

TUTU
Well, not anymore.

Lulu, bug-eyed, looks at Noelani.

TUTU
She'd like you to come home.

NOELANI
See, Lulu? You were terrified that your parents never wanted to see you again. But they haven't forgotten you. And it's only been one day.

TUTU
(speaks gently to Noelani)
And your mother hasn't forgotten you, either. A text came from her ship today. She's trying to get back to see you before school starts.

CLACKING from the doorknocker.

A tall, strong man with stubby brown hair, COLONEL ADAMS, walks in followed by a very pregnant red-haired woman, MRS. ADAMS. Lulu can't decide whether to stare at the woman's enormous belly or her tomato-red hair. The woman understands Lulu's dilemma and smiles at her.

MRS. ADAMS
Aloha. We came to pick up the baby clothes. Are we interrupting?

TUTU
Aloha! Come in. Colonel and Mrs. Adams, this is Lulu Harrison. And, of course, you know Noelani.

Before anyone can answer, they turn in the direction of HEAVY WHEEZING coming from the front door.

LULU
(jumps up)
Watson! You came to get me!

Lulu lunges toward her dog.

Watson, dragging JAMES the DOG BUTLER, toddles into the living room but instead of heaving himself into Lulu's arms, he snuggles up to Mrs. Adams.

LULU
(to Noelani)
Maybe even my dog knows that I'm wanted for poisoning.

MRS. ADAMS
(snuggling Watson)
He probably just smells the papaya ice cream sundae I just ate.

Mrs. Adams rubs her huge baby-filled belly.

I obviously eat all the time.

SCENE 8: LAP IT UP

EXT. KENEKE'S RESTAURANT, ALONG KALANIANAOLE HIGHWAY—TEN MINUTES LATER

Lulu sits on a bench at this roadside restaurant. She eats a bright yellow ice ball that resembles a jumbo sno-cone.

James the Dog Butler gives Lulu a stiff wave as he approaches. He wears his usual outfit, black shorts and a Hawaiian-print shirt under a black sports jacket. A black chauffeur's cap sits sideways over his bald head.

LULU
James! I'm here.

Watson follows James while he acknowledges smiles and stares.

Watson is decked out in the same Hawaiian print shirt as James's and dazzling, ruby-red sunglasses.

JAMES
Watson had to try all twenty-two flavors of shave ice.

LULU
How'd you know which to get him?

JAMES
I can tell what he likes by his lick. He went for guava. They were out of ti-leaf flavor.
(winks at Lulu)

Lulu almost smiles.

LULU
I'm petrified to go home.

James does a little bow and puts out his hand for Lulu to take and get up.

JAMES
I'd say last night you and Watson were perilously close to being left on the doorstep of the local Honolulu dog shelter.

They head toward the Watson Wagon, a shiny black Mercedes station wagon.

LULU
Wait. Watson too?

A TOURIST takes a picture of Watson, who tromps right in front of the camera. He poses by lifting his nose to the left, then to the right. More people with cameras wander over.

> JAMES
> (to Lulu)
> Yes, ma'am. While you were at the set, Watson was back in your kitchen chomping ti leaves off the floor. Pretty soon, everything that was in his stomach came out on either the white furniture or sand-colored carpets.

Lulu halts and stands still as a statue while shave ice melts down her hand.

> JAMES
> Let's just say, Miss Lulu, that last night, I drove from the hospital to the pet emergency room several times.

SCENE 9: MUCKING AROUND

EXT. KANEOHE BAY—NEXT MONDAY MORNING

The Ohana kids wade through waist-high water. They wear snorkel masks. Working in pairs, they pull up killer algae, called *limu*, off an underwater coral reef. If the *limu* isn't removed, the coral reef will die. And that's just the beginning. If the reef dies, the fish, plants, and creepy crawlers that eat, swim, hide, and play in the watery reef world will disappear too.

Lulu and Noelani don't realize it, but they're farther out in the bay from all the other kids.

NOELANI
(bobbing next to Lulu)
My mom learned to be an underwater diver in this bay.

LULU
Your mom's a diver too?

Noelani slides under the water. Lulu follows. Both girls yank fist-fuls of the brown *limu*. Soon they surface and stuff the squishy plant into waterproof sacks slung over their shoulders.

LULU
Your mom might be the coolest mom ever.

Noelani springs off her feet and floats on her back. Lulu bobs onto her back too. The girls stare up at the bright blue sky and watch a wispy cloud glide by.

Lulu flips back to her feet and taps Noelani.

LULU
You're so brave. Your mom is gone for like, months, right?

NOELANI
Usually seven months. But it's always different.

LULU
(suddenly yelling in pain)
AWWWWUUUU!

Lulu bends under the water to examine her leg. It's scraped.

I walked into an edge of the reef.

NOELANI
(looking into the water)
It hurts.

LULU
I know. That coral is so sharp.

NOELANI
(now turns her face toward Lulu)
No. I mean missing my mom. It really hurts.

LULU
You never complain or anything.

NOELANI
I try to not think about or talk about her. But then, ya know what happens? I get more and more shy.

LULU
You're not shy.

NOELANI
You know what I mean. I can't talk in groups. I can't do anything in front of people, like that hula-off. I pretty

121

much know every hula I've ever seen by heart. But when
I try to dance in front of anyone, I can't.

                    LULU
You've just got stage fright!

Noelani sinks underwater and yanks up squirmy algae. Lulu
looks toward the shore.

                    LULU
                  (surprised)
HEY!!

Lulu is splashed from behind. She turns to see Khloe and the
Cs giggling. The three girls are on stand-up paddle boards. They
wear matching zebra-striped bikinis and pink sunglasses.

                    KHLOE
How's the yucky mucky cleanup going?

                    LULU
Aloha, you guys. Don't you have to do algae cleanup?

                    CATE
Nope. We're doing a hula show and our hands have to
be beautiful.

Khloe and the Cs do little swaying hula motions on their paddle
boards. No one tips over!

LULU
(joking tone)
You better be careful not to get blisters from the paddles.
But for me, back to attacking killer algae.

Lulu is about to sink underwater.

KHLOE
Lulu! Make sure you don't serve any killer algae to your
mom and dad's movie crew. I heard you almost ended
everyone's lives.

Lulu sloshes through the water toward the paddle boarders.

LULU
How'd you know? Besides, the good news is, everyone's
fine.

KHLOE
My mom's brother works at the hospital where everyone
went.

LULU
Well, it's no big deal. Noelani and I are even going back to
the set to help this Sunday.

CATE
(looking from Khloe to Carole)
You are?

NOELANI

We are?

LULU
(to Khloe and the Cs)
Sure. Too bad you guys are so busy with hula. Or else
you could come.

Lulu jerks down her face mask and heads toward the shore.
Noelani catches up to her.

NOELANI
Lu, you've got courage, ya know, *koa*, for both of us.

LULU
Actually, now I've got a fib I've got to fix.

Lulu ducks below the surface to wrench up more slimy algae
and figure out how to get her and her pal back onto the *Seas the
Day* set.

SCENE 10: SHOOTING ON FAMILY TIME

**EXT. KUALOA RANCH, SECRET ISLAND BEACH—
SUNDAY, 8 A.M.**

Kualoa Ranch's Secret Island Beach is a real-life tropical paradise. Mangrove and hau trees grow toward the sky just behind
the white sand. Out past the waves rolling onto shore, an island

with a tall, slim peak circled by narrow, flat land rises out of swirling, bright blue water.

Cables snake over the sand. Tall, black cameras, looking like mechanical aliens, perch all around the beach. A dozen people swarm around four tall director's chairs. Fiona stands in the middle and points sharply in different directions. A woman with a makeup brush dabs powder and rubs foundation on the faces of Linc Harrison in a tuxedo and naval officer's cap and the mega skinny actress who's in a red, flowery ball gown. Maxwell rakes the smooth, clean sand so that it looks smoother and cleaner. Alexis, in a white miniskirt and cotton blouse with her apple-green bikini showing through, stands off to the side, trying to look natural as she chats up Maxwell.

Lulu and Noelani sit with their backs up against mangrove tree trunks, well away from the action on the beach.

LULU
I wonder if any koa trees still grow around here?

NOELANI
Maybe.

Lulu picks up a long, yellow pad from the ground. Lulu writes "Koa Tree" with an orange pencil.

Watson, sporting doggie board shorts pulled up over a chunky diaper and a red shirt that says "LIFEGUARD," sleeps a few feet away.

                    LULU
              (tapping her pencil)
Maybe I should ask my mom to add a line in the script
about koa trees?

Both girls look up to see Fiona holding two cell phones, one to
each ear.

                    LULU
But I don't think this is a good time to talk to her.

Lulu reaches into her tote bag, grabs a handful of taro chips, and
drops them in the lap of her orange skirt. She pulls out a glass
jar of mango salsa. She offers the jar to Noelani and then dips
and crunches herself.

                  NOELANI
Lu, how'd you get her to let us come to the set today?

Lulu leans the back of her head against the tree trunk.

                    LULU
I patched over my lie with the truth.

                  NOELANI
Good plan. How?

                    LULU
I got a gigantic break that they were filming on location.
I told Mom that I could really be helpful on the set today
because I've learned so much about Hawaiian trees and

plants that if anyone watched her movie and wanted to know what a plant or tree was called, she could know. That's why I'm writing everything down, so I can give her a list.

The girls watch as Fiona waves her hand and says something in Alexis's direction. Alexis un-poses herself and walks away from Maxwell who re-scrapes the perfect sand.

> NOELANI
> (tiny smile playing on her lips)
> Looks like your mom had a moment to talk with Alexis.

> LULU
> (giggling)
> Looks like Lex just got busted for ooogling Maxwell.

> NOELANI
> He seems nice.

> LULU
> (shakes her head)
> He is, but his dad's some famous Shakespeare actor who's furious that he's off making Hollywood movies on the beaches of Hawaii.

> NOELANI
> (cracking up)
> How do you even know all that?

LULU

That's the kind of stuff they all mostly talk about. If they're ever home.

Lulu dunks another chip, but it accidentally sinks in the mango salsa jar.

Noelani gets more chips from Lulu's bag.

NOELANI

I can't even believe we're eating taro chips at eight a.m.

Lulu gets up and crouches near Watson. She straightens his fuchsia-and-orange sunglasses and feeds him crushed taro chips. He gobbles them.

LULU

Well, this is about the latest my parents have gone to work all week. We were lucky it was only six a.m. when we had to wake up to go with them.

NOELANI

Getting up this early doesn't feel like summer vacation.

LULU

Every day this week they had to come out here at five in the morning and shoot so my mom would get direct morning sunlight.

QUIET ON THE SET, PLEASE! ALL, QUIET ON THE SET!
drifts up to the girls from the Assistant Director's bullhorn.

Noelani shifts her back against the tree trunk so she faces Lulu.

NOELANI
(whispering)
You could go closer to the action.
(her eyes glance down toward the beach)
You don't have to hide back here with me.

Lulu returns and sits down next to Noelani. Their backs lean
against the same tree trunk.

LULU

I begged my way to get this close and am doing exactly
what my parents said. I'm staying put and writing down
the names of trees and plants. The ONLY reason I'd go
down there would be if a tidal wave was coming and I
could save people from being swept away.

Just then, a wild CHICKEN darts out of the mangrove and hau
tree forest. It cackles and scampers toward Secret Island Beach.
As if a lightning bolt struck his tail, Watson jerks to his feet and
chugs after the bird. His sturdy stubby legs work as hard as they
can. His sunglasses tumble off.

Lulu scrambles to her feet and tears off after Watson.

                        LULU
                      (shouts)
Watson, NO!

The chicken clucks its head off while it half flies, half runs a
frantic, curly path toward the perfectly raked sand. Watson is fast
on the chicken's tail feathers. Lulu runs after him as best as she
can while trying not to slip and lose her ALOHA hat bouncing
on her head. As they approach the set, Maxwell steps in front
of the chicken so that it swerves and darts back up toward the
trees. Watson turns after it. Lulu, however, gets the tip of her
left shoe caught in a cable and face-plants on the perfect sand.

              ASSISTANT DIRECTOR'S VOICE
      CUT!

The handsome, grinning Maxwell offers Lulu his hand and
helps her up.

                        LULU
              (wiping sand from her lips)
        Oh, I'm so sorry!

Alexis approaches.

                       ALEXIS
                     (sneering)
      You're way pathetic and so in trouble.

Panting, Watson returns and lies down next to Lulu. She grabs
his collar, but in a moment, he wiggles away. He heaves himself

toward the scent of breakfast sandwiches being served a few feet away. He smashes into the skinny actress, who drenches herself with coffee she was sipping. Watson leaps at the food table but doesn't get high enough off the ground. Instead, he bangs into the table's leg and sends silver serving dishes clattering to the ground. Watson snatches bacon from the ground and runs for the trees.

Everyone on the set freezes. Lulu lingers on the sand, not sure she can find the courage to move.

LULU
(to Alexis)
This wasn't my fault, exactly. I'll apologize to Mom.

ALEXIS
I wouldn't do that if I were you.

Lulu looks over to her mother. An ASSISTANT wearing a headset holds out a phone. Fiona takes it. She cocks her head. Smiles. Nods. Laughs sweetly. Shakes her head. She hands the phone back to the waiting assistant and then walks about ten feet away. Linc walks over to her.

Lulu and Alexis wander toward their parents. They overhear.

FIONA
(quiet but angry)
Sanyo will be here in twenty minutes!
(loses her usual calm and yells)
And my set has turned into a circus!

Lulu and Alexis swiftly back away from their parents.

131

LULU
(quietly to Alexis)
Maybe I'll apologize some other time.

SCENE 11: UNDERWATER

EXT. WATER'S EDGE, HANAUMA BAY—MONDAY MORNING

Hanauma Bay, a horseshoe-shaped bay, used to be the private fishing spot for the Hawaiian royal family. More than 30,000 years ago, coral reefs formed here, and so this safe bay became a natural home for zillions of colorful fish and animals. But after hundreds of years of fishing, Hanauma Bay was turning into a fishy ghost town. Now, the whole bay is protected. The fish and everything living are safe to swim, crawl, wiggle, and not be caught.

The Ohana Camp kids gather around Uncle Akamu and Auntie Moana. The kids are decked out in bathing suits, snorkel masks, and flippers. Lulu, of course, wears her SPF 50 pants and shirt over a bathing suit and a bathing cap squeezed over her wild, shaggy hair.

KENNA
(to Lulu next to her)
Is it true that snorkeling here is like swimming in a fish tank?

LULU

I've never been in a fish tank, but I think it's like swimming in a warm bathtub.

UNCLE AKAMU

Keike, listen. My three rules and then you go with the fish. *Ekahi*, one: buddy system in the water. No one swims alone. *Elua*, two: don't step on the reef. You'll slice yourself AND crunch any living thing you step on. And *ekolu*, three: absolutely NO *opala*, no trash of any kind, on this sand or in the water. That means no bathroom in this living underwater palace.

KAPONO

What if I have to, ummmm, go?

He lifts his leg, pretending he's a doggie making a pee.

AUNTIE MOANA

You take off the flippers and walk on your big feet to the restrooms.

Kids chuckle.

LIAM

I have a question.
    (looks at Lulu)
What happened with you and Watson on your parents' movie yesterday?

Lulu looks at Noelani who shakes her head no. Liam notices.

133

LIAM

Noelani didn't tell me. Khloe's mom knows my mom and told her about it.

Lulu slunks onto the sand.

LULU

Geez peas. You guys, I was just helping my mom by writing down names of plants and trees on location when Watson took off. He crashed up the set.

KENNA and KAPONO

Uh-oh!

NOELANI
(to Lulu)
And he drenched the actress.

LULU

Yeah. He made the lead actress spill coffee on her ball gown.

Ohana kids shake their heads sadly.

LULU

The worst part is, I really just wanted to help. *Seas the Day* isn't going too well and I keep making everything worse.

MALEKO
(drumming on his fingers on his snorkel mask)
Hey. Lulu. Don't feel bad. I get in trouble, like, all the
time for stupid stuff.

Heads nod.

Kids start chatting at once. Everyone has a story about causing
mischief and getting busted.

HUUROOO. The sound from Uncle Akamu's conch shell gets
their attention.

UNCLE AKAMU
Now, let's go swimming!

The kids scramble toward the water. Lulu, in her flippers, moves
like a duckling taking its first steps. Uncle Akamu walks among
the kids and explains habits of certain fish and where they might
be found in the bay.

LULU
I want to see a turtle!

UNCLE AKAMU
Honu, the sea turtles, are shy and rare. Almost extinct.
Hard to see.

Lulu SPLATS onto the sand just before the water. She's so
close that when the wavelets lap onto the shore, sea froth licks
the top of her bathing cap. Noelani smiles. Lulu waves to

show she's still alive and crawls the last few feet into the bluest turquoise water.

EXT. IN THE WATER, HANAUMA BAY—FORTY-FIVE MINUTES LATER

Lulu yanks her snorkel tube from her mouth. Noelani comes up to the surface and flips out her snorkel.

> LULU
> Do we have to go back to shore soon?

Noelani checks her watch.

> NOELANI
> Yes.

Lulu shoves the snorkel back into her mouth.

> LULU
> Gheeees peeeees. Ahhh ghaaa tahhh fuuund hooohnooo.

Noelani waves her hand.

> NOELANI
> What?

Lulu tugs the mouthpiece out just enough to speak.

> LULU
> I said, geeeeez peas! I gotta find a *honu*!

Noelani grabs Lulu's arm before she plunges down.

NOELANI
I have an idea. Let's just drift, kinda around one place.

LULU
(pulling out the mouthpiece again)
You mean not swim around? OK, let's go to the shallower
water near the reefs.

Noelani gives Lulu a thumbs-up and drops underwater.

Lulu lifts her feet off the sea bottom and puts her face into the water.

 CUT!! Super quick! You know how in a movie, you sometimes see what the main character is seeing? As if you're in their shoes? It's called a Point of View shot and written POV in the script. It puts the camera where the main character is, so you're watching what their eyes would be seeing. I'm gonna try it. Now back to: ACTION!!

LULU'S POV: A green-blue watery world of reef mountains and kelp forests seems endless. Rays of sunlight dance through the water. An animal kingdom of fish swims free. Parrot fish, goatfish, butterflyfish, and raccoon butterflyfish flick their fins and glide around showing off dazzling neon colors not found in any animals on land.

Lulu and Noelani drift in the current, half floating and half dogpaddling. They pretend to be mermaids, lost in a world far away from their own.

Just when they imagine they are sleeping in the liquid deep, Lulu sees it!

He's oddly shaped compared to the fish, but he's graceful. The sea turtle, a *honu*, swims within ten feet of Lulu and Noelani. His flippers and head look small compared to his big, oval shell. Lulu and Noelani exchange a quick glance at each other, eyes wide inside their masks. They watch the *honu* surface for air and then glide past them. His eyes stare at them for a moment. He's not scared. Just curious.

EXT. HANAUMA BAY SHORE—FIFTEEN MINUTES LATER

Lulu crawls out of the water just as she crawled in. Noelani bounds out, comfortable in flippers as if they were her feet. Uncle Akamu meets them.

LULU
(speaking extra fast)

We saw one! A *honu*! She or, well, maybe he wore a darkish olive-brown shell and floated and drifted with that big, heavy shell on its back.

The twins rush over.

KENNA

You saw a *honu*?

LULU

Yeah. He had flippers for feet and hands. And his skin was greenish and leathery.

Kapono wiggles his fingers in his sister's face.

KAPONO

Like a martian.

Lulu, still on her hands and knees, flops onto her bottom and tugs off her flippers. Uncle Akamu sits down next to her.

LULU
(looks at Uncle Akamu)

You know what?

Uncle Akamu doesn't respond. He stares out at the bay.

LULU

That honu wasn't scared of me. She didn't even pull her head into her shell and hide.

Lulu scrunches down her chin and neck and shrugs up her shoulders like a turtle pulling in its head inside a shell.

UNCLE AKAMU
(not taking his eyes off the water)

Honu can't pull their heads in. That's only land turtles.

LULU

Oh. Well, she looked right at me. She had little black eyes.
I felt like she was trying to tell me something.

Uncle Akamu and Lulu sit quietly for a few moments.

UNCLE AKAMU

Sea turtles are believed to symbolize great navigators,
who always find their way home again and again.

LULU

Even if the sea is rough and the water is murky?

Uncle Akamu grins.

UNCLE AKAMU

Yes, Lulu, even then.

SCENE 12: IT'LL BE A BLAST

**INT. HARRISON HOUSE ENTRANCE, LIVING ROOM
AND *LANAI*—WEDNESDAY AFTERNOON**

Lulu approaches the front door.

MAYA
(points to Lulu's feet)

Shoes.

Lulu kicks off her grimy, damp shoes.

MAYA
(points to side of the house)
Then shower.

LULU
Why are there so many trucks in the driveway? It's like the whole house needs to be repaired on the same day at the same time.

MAYA
That's your sister. She's planning a party with a fireworks show.

LULU
A WHAT?

MAYA
Maybe you want to talk to her about it.

LULU
(lets out a long sigh)
Talking to Lex about a party is a scary idea.

Lulu races off to the outdoor shower…and to snoop on Alexis's plans.

A stocky, super-tan man walks toward Lulu. He carries a large plastic box filled with various sizes of colorfully wrapped packages. He wears a black shirt with "PELE" written in yellow across the front.

LULU

Excuse me, uuuuumm, Pele?

The man stops.

PELE MAN 1
(grunts out a greeting)
Ya think my name's Pele? HA! That's funny. And so is his and his and his.

The man gestures with his chin toward other men around the huge backyard.

Lulu sees men measuring the ground, rolling out cables, hammering tent poles, and unstacking chairs. Up on the *lanai*, Alexis lies on a chaise, talking on her cell phone.

LULU

Oh. Is Pele the name of your company or something? I didn't know that. But I learned at my Ohana Camp that Pele is the Hawaiian name for the Volcano God.

PELE MAN 1

Smart kid.

Lulu zooms up the *lanai* steps. Alexis punches off her call.

LULU

Lex, what's going on?

ALEXIS
(thrilled with herself)
Très exciting. Mom put *moi* in charge of a cast and crew party. Right here at our house.

LULU
A what? For what?

ALEXIS
Well, partly thanks to you, *Seas the Day* is even more behind schedule than ever. The actors are grouchy about working so much. The crew protests every day. Mom thought a party would lift everyone's spirits.

LULU
I wanna help.

ALEXIS
You can't get near this event.

PELE MAN 1
(walking by with a measuring tape)
How close to this *lanai* do ya want the fireworks? We're gonna light up this place like a Christmas tree.

LULU
But it's the middle of summer! Not Christmas. And what about all the *hokus*, ya know, the stars?

Watson, wearing a T-shirt that says "COCONUT" and has an

arrow pointing in the direction of his head, sniffs a box of sparklers on the ground near Alexis.

PELE MAN 2

The *hokus* will be a little less bright the night we light these babies!

He shakes rockets he's holding.

Lulu lies down on the ground next to Watson.

LULU

What's so bad about just leaving the glowing stars?

ALEXIS

How can you be against fireworks? That's like totally un-American.

Lulu sits up.

LULU

How can you be against bright stars? That's totally un-Hawaiian. For your information, ancient Polynesians paddled canoes across the ocean to Hawaii just by navigating with stars.

ALEXIS

Not sure what that has to do with a fab Hollywood-style party in Hawaii.

A CARPENTER approaches.

144

CARPENTER
(to Alexis)
Miss Harrison, where do you want the stage?

LULU
A stage? Who's performing?

ALEXIS
Fiona and Linc are going to thank Mr. Sanyo.

LULU
THE boss of Sanyo Studios is going to be HERE?

ALEXIS
Yup. And he'll probably say a few words also.
(to Carpenter)
How about putting the stage by the pool? We can reflect some lights off the water.

LULU
Hey, is there any way my Ohana friends can come perform and Uncle Akamu and Caridyn can play music? I bet Mr. Sanyo and the *Seas the Day* people have never seen such amazing local talent.

ALEXIS
(sarcastic tone)
I'm sure they haven't!

CARPENTER
Hey, I know Akamu! We fish together. He's good! He can

catch an octopus with his bare hands and kill it without causing it any pain by popping its head inside out.

Alexis shoves her sunglasses to the top of her head.

ALEXIS
Way, hyper gross. Not AT ALL the vibe we're going for here.

Sliding her perfectly blue polished toes into her Christian Louboutin blue-and-white striped canvas wedges, Alexis walks to the pool with the Carpenter.

Lulu follows.

LULU
Lex, my friends might like the fireworks show. I'm really thinking: how about we do this party together. Remember my birthday we did together?!

Alexis spins around and glares at Lulu.

ALEXIS
There's a difference between YOUR birthday and Fiona's cast and crew party. This is for Mom's work!

Lulu skulks back to the *lanai* and bounces down onto a springy chaise to think.

Suddenly, whimpering and moaning come from Watson. Lulu rolls onto the ground and pulls Watson close. Then she sees…!

LULU
(calls out)
Lex! Peles!! Hurry! I think Watson's eaten the sparklers!!

Lulu pulls away shreds of blue wrapper stuck with saliva around Watson's mouth.

Alexis and Pele 1 peer down at Lulu and Watson.

ALEXIS
(holding in a laugh)
See, he's into MY kind of party spirit.

PELE MAN 1
(snorting a loud laugh)
And next time that dog farts, he's gonna have flames coming from under his tail.

SCENE 13: MALL-ZILLA

EXT. ALA MOANA CENTER–FRIDAY AFTERNOON

This is the largest mall in Hawaii and just about the world. Stores jam each of the giant four levels. Every floor opens to the sky. Birds fly through and sunlight streams in. Shoppers bustle from one crowded shop to another.

Alexis leads Lulu up to Level Three. She's here to shop for the *Seas the Day* party and nothing is going to slow her down.

LULU

How long do we have to be here? I want to catch Mom
and Dad at home before they go out tonight and ask them
how I can help with the party.

ALEXIS

There's nothing you need to talk to them about. Here's
my list:
(plucks her iPhone from her tiny silver purse and reads from
the screen)
Party favors. Matching Hawaiian shirts for the band and
waiters. A party dress for *moi*—

Alexis SLAMS into Khloe. Her iPhone CLATTERS to the
ground and SKITTERS to a stop as it heads UP an escalator.

KHLOE

(not recognizing Alexis)
Watch where you're going!

CATE

Yeah!

CAROLE

Text and walk often?

Khloe and the Cs snigger among themselves.

LULU

Aloha, guys! Why are you dressed up for hula?

> KHLOE

We're performing here.

Alexis recognizes Khloe and the Cs instantly.

> ALEXIS

If you girls weren't sashaying around in hula skirts, maybe you'd watch where YOU were going.

> LULU

Geez peas!

Lulu points to the escalator carrying Alexis's iPhone up. No one notices. Alexis continues arguing with Khloe.

Lulu chases the iPhone up the escalator. She ends up on the TOP floor. She stoops down to pick up the un-cracked phone.

"CALIFORNIA GIRLS" song plays from Alexis's phone. The name MAXWELL flashes on the screen along with a red heart.

> LULU
> (to herself)

That's a call I'm not gonna take.

SCENE 14: GETTING A BRIGHT IDEA

EXT. ALA MOANA CENTER—FIVE MINUTES LATER

ALEXIS

Hand over the phone, Lu.

LULU

How about *mahalo* for rescuing it?

Lulu drops it in Alexis's outstretched hand.

ALEXIS

How about those girls can't be bigger weenies! They're doing a hula performance here this afternoon. If I have to see them shake around, I'll gag, so I've got to get my stuff done fast.

Alexis quickly clicks her Gucci slides down the corridor. Lulu jogs to catch her.

LULU

Ya know, Lex, my best Ohana friend, Noelani, hulas way better than they do.

Alexis stops and looks at Lulu. She props her sunglasses on the top of her head and stares at Lulu.

ALEXIS

I have exactly zero interest in judging "So You Think You Can Dance—the Hula Episode."

 CUT!! I am just about to have the MOST boring two hours of my life. Alexis drags me along to about a zillion stores and is too busy to notice if

I'm still breathing. To spare you the loneliness of my sister time with Alexis, I'm going to write what's called a MONTAGE. I bet you've seen it tons of times in movies. It's when you get a quick shot of different things happening that express a similar idea. Here you go:

MONTAGE—ALEXIS AND LULU SHOP FOR THE PARTY

★ Alexis buys 100 Hawaii print LeSportsac bags. Lulu sits near the store entrance reading.

★ Alexis holds up two different Hawaiian shirts. Lulu points to one. Alexis buys twenty of the other.

★ Alexis bursts out of a dressing room wearing a tropical-print miniskirt and black-fringed bikini top. Lulu slumps on the floor eating taro chips and salsa from her tote bag.

★ Alexis and Lulu sit at a long table at a fancy restaurant. Small plates filled with tasting portions of different foods cover the table. Alexis points to dishes and the head of the restaurant writes it down. Lulu eats the food left on any plate that's in her reach.

BACK TO MALL

Lulu drags her feet. Both girls are heavy with shopping bags. Strains of hula music start to play.

ALEXIS
Step on it, Lulu. I could break out in hives if I catch as much as a glimpse of those ninnies dancing.

LULU
(plunking down shopping bags)
I shouldn't tell you this, but nothing would make Khloe and the Cs more mega-mad than if my Ohana pals came and performed at the *Seas the Day* party.

ALEXIS
(to herself)
Nothing would make me happier than putting those girls in their place.
(to Lulu)
OK, Lu. Deal. But I need a written list of what everyone's performing and doing. And the whole gang of you only has ten minutes, TOPS.

LULU
I promise! You won't be disappointed.

SCENE 15: HAWAII'S GOT TALENT

EXT. BELLOWS BEACH—THURSDAY AFTERNOON

Bellows Beach is peaceful and quiet. It's on military land, and the only way to use the beach during the week is to come with someone in the military or be in the military yourself. Since Uncle Akamu, his two brothers, and his father served in the United States Navy, Uncle Akamu can come to Bellows Beach anytime.

Gigantic ironwood trees grow close to the sand, so there's tons of shade. The Ohana Camp gang has the beach pretty much to themselves. They sit at picnic benches under the trees and finish plate lunches of *huli-huli* chicken (grilled BBQ chicken), macaroni salad, and french fries.

> LIAM
>
> Hey, Lulu, what time should I be at your house? I'm psyched 'cause my ukulele plucking is getting really good.

> MALEKO
> (drumming straws on the picnic table)
> I wanna get there early to see where I'll be drumming.

> LULU
>
> There's gonna be a stage. Alexis has it set up so it's floating in the pool.

> KENNA
>
> What time do we come watch the fireworks?

> KAPONO
> (to his sister)
> You're scared of fireworks!

Pretending to set off a firework, Kapono tosses a shredded napkin in his sister's face.

> KAPONO
>
> KAAAAPOW!!

Lulu guzzles pineapple Waialua soda.

LULU

Alexis hasn't told me yet when everyone should come, and I haven't seen my parents at home in days, so I can't ask them.

AUNTIE MOANA

Lulu, just let us all know when we should come and when we should leave. We know this is an important party for your mother and father's work.

KENNA

Kapono and I have been practicing our song every night. Our mom says our voices are blending perfectly.

KAPONO

But since we're singing at your house, we can't sing at a YMCA talent show.

Lulu puts down her soda.

LULU

Why not?

KENNA and KAPONO

It's the same night.

Lulu frowns.

AUNTIE MOANA

That's OK. There will be other competitions. Uncle Akamu and Caridyn turned down performing at the Royal Hawaiian Hotel *luau* that night.

UNCLE AKAMU
There'll always be another *luau*!

MALEKO
Yeah! And the Jack Johnson concert.

LIAM
(to Maleko)
You're not using your Jack Johnson tickets?

MALEKO
Why? You want them?

LIAM
(chewing fries)
No. I'm going to Lulu's with everyone.
(swallows and lowers his voice)
I actually canceled a date with Khloe.

Maleko stops drumming and looks at his friend.

LIAM
And, man, can she yell loud!

Liam picks up a fry and tosses it at Maleko. It misses and lands on Noelani's plate. Lulu plucks it off and eats it.

LULU
Noe, you haven't touched your food.

                    NOELANI
                  (in a whisper)
I'm way too petrified to dance hula at your parents'
big party.

                     LULU
Sure you can. You're the best hula-er in America.

                    NOELANI
Maybe I can hula, but I'm not brave. I have no *koa*,
remember? When you guys started talking about a stage
and all, I thought I would faint.

French fries fly past Lulu and Noelani. Liam and Maleko started
a fry food fight. Most land on the ground near Watson, who had
been sunning himself but quickly morphs into a furry vacuum.

                    KAPONO
              (panting like he's a dog)
   Look at that fat little pug!

Watson's T-shirt that says "THE BOSS" seems to stretch tighter
by the fry.

Auntie Moana walks over.

                  AUNTIE MOANA
Finish up and let's go down to the beach before the
wind whips up and the clouds come in. It's gonna be
overcast soon.

Lulu and Noelani dump their trash and head toward the ocean. Watson, too full to waddle himself, rides on Lulu's boogie board while she tugs him along.

EXT. BELLOWS BEACH, NEAR THE SHORELINE—FIVE MINUTES LATER

Lulu sits under her orange beach umbrella. She pulls her ALOHA cap brim down so low on her face she can barely see. She's yanked the sleeves of her SPF 50 shirt over her wrists. If a ray of sun hits her skin, it would be a miracle. Noelani lies on a thin, faded blue-and-white-striped beach towel. Her eyes are closed. Her warm, brown skin welcomes the sunshine.

> NOELANI
>
> I practice every night. I actually hula with my eyes closed and think of the story I'm telling with my hands. But every time I open my eyes, everything about me freezes.

> LULU
>
> (worried)
>
> Are you saying that you're not going to come?

> NOELANI
>
> (opens her eyes and looks at Lulu)
>
> Lu, my mom's supposed to Skype me from her ship Saturday night. It's been set up through her central command.

Lulu looks at Noelani, confused.

                    NOELANI
Central command is like the highest level of her bosses
who approve that stuff.

                     LULU
What stuff?

                    NOELANI
Like talking to your daughter and when you get to come
home and see her.

Lulu puts her sandy, sweaty hand on her friend's shoulder.

                     LULU
Geez peas! When you talk to your mom Saturday, tell her
to come home soon, so I can meet her before summer
ends 'cause I need to tell her how sweet and fantabulous
her daughter is!

 CUT!! More than anything, I'd want my best of all
Hawaiian friends to be at my parents' party with me.
She's an amazing dancer and watching her would,
for sure, have all the people working on *Seas the Day*
forget their hard work and enjoy something beautiful. BUT if
there's anyone who understands wanting to get a minute (or two)
with your mom, it's me, Lulu! So, the show will have to go on
without Noelani. OK, back to: ACTION!!

SCENE 16: PUG RESCUE

EXT. SHORELINE, BELLOWS BEACH—CONTINUOUS

TIGHT SHOT on Watson as he lies asleep on Lulu's boogie board.

The warm midday sun, the smell of french fry grease, and his full belly lull the pug into a deep snooze.

WIDE SHOT of Ohana kids splashing along the shore, boogie boarding, or body surfing in the ocean.

CLOSE-UP again on Watson. Waves move closer and closer to the foam board and then begin to lap the front edge. Soon, the warm Pacific Ocean surf pulls the boogie board with the sleepy pug on it out to sea!!

CUT TO: Lulu and Noelani deep in conversation about how hard it can be to get your mother to notice you're alive. Lulu sticks her hand into her I USED TO BE A PLASTIC BAG tote and pulls out a two *li hing mui* lollipops.

LULU
(holding both out to Noelani)
Whale or heart? Even Watson is hooked on them. He and I share lick for lick.

> NOELANI

Sharing is caring.

Lulu glances around her.

> LULU

Where's Watson?!!

Noelani springs up.

> NOELANI

He probably dragged himself back to the picnic tables to hunt for fries.

> LULU

No. I dragged him down here on my boogie board. He was so stuffed from lunch, there's no way he would've waddled off.

Noelani puts her hand over her brow to keep the sun from her eyes and scans the beach.

> LULU
> (cups her hands around her mouth)

WATSON!!!

Most of her voice is carried away by the strong winds blowing off the ocean.

Lulu instinctively runs toward the rolling surf. Noelani bolts after her.

LULU
(to Noelani)

He hates the WATER!

NOELANI

I know.

LULU

And doesn't even like fish. Well, except for extra-cheesy Goldfish crackers.

NOELANI

I know. I've seen him eat a whole bag of those.

LULU

And he doesn't know how to swim.

NOELANI

I know.

LULU

And I didn't put his dog floaties on!!

NOELANI

I know. You always slide them on his legs in case he gets too close to the ocean.

By the time they reach the wet, squishy sand, several Ohana kids stand together pointing out to sea. Lulu staggers toward them.

LIAM
Hey, man. I think that's Watson out there!

Lulu, panting from her run across the sand, SPLASHES into the crash of the breaking waves. She swims quickly toward Watson. Liam and Noelani swim after her.

CLOSE-UP on Watson, who peels open his eyes and quickly closes them. He decides to play dead and not move. Even twitching his stubby tail could cause the board to wiggle.

CUT BACK TO: Lulu. She is exhausted and gulps for breath, though she swallows more salt water than air. Noelani and Liam try to reach Lulu, but she's too far ahead.

SPLISH, SPLOSH, SPLISH, SPLOSH.

Lulu turns at the sound and sees two HEADS. Arms circle above the choppy ocean surface and disappear back under it, again and again like pinwheels spinning in the wind. Heads and arms move fast despite the rise and fall of the swells.

As the swimmers get closer, one head pops out. It's close enough for Lulu to see.

UNCLE AKAMU
Just FLOAT. Relax.

He does a fast breaststroke over to her.

He's up to Lulu in two strokes. His left arm, like a steel cable, wraps her from behind and holds her head up.

> UNCLE AKAMU
> (his voice is calm)
> *Aloha.* Now. I'm gonna let go of you for one second because I'm gonna take off my shirt. Got it?

Lulu nods and sputters out salty water at the same time.

> UNCLE AKAMU
> (voice is playful)
> Now I know you're wondering, why is Uncle taking off his beautiful T-shirt here in the ocean? It's already soaking wet and Auntie's gonna kill him if it's ruined.

Lulu nods again.

> UNCLE AKAMU
> Well, I'm gonna pull it off and you're gonna grab it. OK? I'm gonna hold the other side and I'm gonna tow you in.

Lulu splashes her right hand. She wants Akamu's attention.

> LULU
> Wahh...
> (spits out water)
> ...t-son.

UNCLE AKAMU
(smiling)
He's in good hands. He's being rescued by a United
States Marine.

Lulu tries to turn around to look at Uncle Akamu, but he's
taken the moment to pull his sopping-wet shirt over his head.
Within seconds, he hands one end to Lulu and begins towing
her toward shore.

ANGLE: BEACH

Lulu and Uncle Akamu reach the shore. Lulu crawls through the
mushy sand to Auntie Moana, who lifts her up and wraps her in a
towel. Noelani and all the Ohana kids form a huddle around her.

KAPONO
Hurry! Get Lulu some of her mango salsa and taro chips
to revive her.

He exaggerates a goofy run and wails like a siren.

All giggle a bit nervously, but it releases some of the fear.

KENNA
She needs one of her famous coconut shakes.

NOELANI
Actually, someone go to Lulu's backpack and get her a *li
hing mui* lollipop.

Maleko halts his right hand that had been tapping beats on his left forearm and sprints up to Lulu's bag.

LULU
(croaking)
Watson. You guys?! I lost my puggie.

Suddenly, a VOICE booms above the kids' heads.

VOICE
No, ma'am. You haven't.

The huddle around Lulu parts to reveal a tall, muscular MAN with short, brown stubble on his head and a waterlogged pug tossed over his broad, strong right shoulder.

COLONEL ADAMS
At your service, ma'am. Colonel Ben Adams! I believe this sack of pug-tatoes belongs to you.

The kids laugh. Auntie Moana and Uncle Akamu smile. Lulu gathers her reserve energy and gallops toward Colonel Adams. He slides the pug off his shoulder and into Lulu's arms.

LULU
(tears run down her cheeks)
Oh, Colonel, I don't know what to, I mean...right now it's hard to know if I'm crying or just leaking salt water.

Colonel Adams laughs.

COLONEL ADAMS

That's good. I like that. What's your name?

LULU

Lulu, sir.

COLONEL ADAMS

Lulu? Didn't I meet you at Lieutenant Colonel Nui's house?

NOELANI

(trying to be heard and disappear at the same time)

Aloha, Colonel. *Mahalo* for helping my friend.

COLONEL ADAMS

(warm friendly voice)

Noelani, any friend of yours is a friend of mine. And, hey, I think your mom's going to be calling you this weekend.

NOELANI

(too embarrassed to speak, whispers)

Mahalo.

LULU

Colonel, ummm, sir! How can I thank you?!

COLONEL ADAMS

Well, you could let me keep this.

He pulls something out of the waistband of his board shorts. It's Lulu's ALOHA cap.

COLONEL ADAMS

Top of my head was getting scorched out here. My wife will kill me if I come home with my noggin sunburned. She always tells me to cover it up.

LULU

My hat!

Colonel Adams puts the ALOHA baseball cap on.

COLONEL ADAMS

What do you guys think?

Even though it looks hysterical to see the tall, muscle-y man wearing the red-and-white cap with the rainbow heart for the *O* in ALOHA, everyone tells him that he looks great. No one's messing with this Marine!

LULU

It might look better on you than it did on me!

Colonel Adams tips his head in respect to Akamu and begins to walk away. He quickly stops and turns back.

COLONEL ADAMS

Lulu! Give that dog of yours swimming lessons! That's an order!

Colonel Adams salutes the Ohana Camp gang and heads toward his blanket on the sand.

SCENE 17: LIGHT UP MY LIFE

EXT. HARRISON HOUSE GROUNDS AND *LANAI*—ONE HOUR LATER

Cables and thick black cords lie around the ground like sleeping snakes. Ladders rest along the *lanai* railing. Boxes of colored floodlights, strings of tiny white lights, and black electrical tape are piled onto the outdoor dining table.

Alexis, in a red string bikini top and red-and-white floral-print shorts that button just below her tiny waist and end at the tippy top of her tanned legs, gives instructions from the edge of the *lanai*.

A soggy, exhausted Lulu staggers onto the *lanai*. She holds Watson, who's wrapped in a fleece blanket. Scraps of *huli-huli* chicken stick around his mouth. Clearly, he's been given an extra meal to help him over his near-death experience.

> LULU
>
> Lex, I'm finally home.

Alexis doesn't turn. She continues pointing and yelling.

> LULU
> (louder)
>
> Lex! I made it.

Alexis spins around and looks at Lulu.

ALEXIS

Wow, Lu. You OK? You look like you just survived a shipwreck.

Alexis sits down next to Lulu on a chaise. She loops her long, thin arm around Lulu's waist and squeezes her little sister. Alexis's silver bangles cut into Lulu's clammy skin.

ALEXIS
(stares at Lulu for a moment)
Whatever happened must have been serious because you're not wearing that disgusting, grungy ALOHA cap.

LULU
(speaks super fast)
Well, that would be because I gave it to Colonel Adams, who saved Watson from a watery death.

ALEXIS
Hmmm. You think I can make a sequel that ends differently?

The sisters laugh.

LULU
(serious again)
He found my hat churning around in the waves that crashed on me and almost dunked me to my doom.

ALEXIS
(violet eyes sparkle)
So in my sequel, the hero gets a box of ALOHA caps if he
leaves the dog in the ocean.

Lulu mock punches her sister in the shoulder.

ALEXIS
Glad you're here. I need your help deciding where all the
colored lights should go in the trees.

LULU
Glad you're asking me about lights 'cause I've wanted to
tell you that the lights should be solar.

A UPS MAN wheels out a dolly stacked with two huge card-
board boxes. The boxes bounce and slide every time the dolly
bumps over the cords. Alexis leaps up on her very tall red Miu
Miu shoes. Lulu follows.

LULU
What are these?

Alexis teeters forward on her heels and hovers over the UPS
Man, who's lifting off the boxes.

The UPS Man cuts open a box. Alexis reaches in and yanks out
a handful of leis with animal prints.

ALEXIS
Aren't these the grooviest party accessories?!

LULU

Plastic leis?!

ALEXIS

Not plastic. Polyester.

Lulu peers inside the box.

LULU

My head's fuzzy from just almost drowning in the Pacific Ocean, but let me get this straight. You ordered fake leis from China for a party in Hawaii, the state known worldwide for real flower leis and lei making?

CRASH! THUD! CLONK!!

For a second, there's no noise. Lulu and Alexis dash to the edge of the *lanai* and look over the railing. They see a wide, heavyset man on the ground, tangled in sticks and leaves. He's the ELECTRICIAN.

ELECTRICIAN

I'm cool. Just grabbed a branch that couldn't hold my girlish figure. Haa haaa!

The Electrician gets to his feet. He must weigh about two hundred pounds. He begins to climb up the ladder.

LULU
(calling down to him)

WAIT!

(to Alexis)
Why do all the lights have to be in the trees?

The Electrician thuds up the stairs and clonks across the *lanai*. Twigs stick out of his hair, and leaves and flowers cling to his shirt.

ELECTRICIAN
(to Alexis)
Look, miss, I wanna get these lights hung.

LULU
Isn't there any way all these lights can hang on something else? Ya know, instead of trees?

ALEXIS
(nodding toward Lulu)
My sandy, damp little sis here is one of America's biggest tree huggers. She—

ELECTRICIAN
Yeah. Well, there're overhead rigs and C-stands. Ya know, like they use for lighting movie sets.

LULU and ALEXIS
Perfect.

ELECTRICIAN
Well, hanging that way is way more money.

LULU
(to Electrician)
What if you used solar lights? How much would that cost?

ELECTRICIAN
(thinks a moment)
Actually, less. I wouldn't have to run all the cable. The bulbs would just power up from the sunlight that they'd store during the day.

ALEXIS
(to Electrician)
Then let's do that.

LULU
Lex! I'm really helping! I'm saving the movie money.

SCENE 18: PARTY 411

INT. HARRISONS' ENTRY HALL—SATURDAY, 8 A.M.

Rain pelts the house. Sheets of water slide down the floor-to-ceiling glass *lanai* doors that Lulu can never remember seeing shut. Lulu sits in a poufy vanilla-colored chair and stares outside. She wears orange pajamas. Her hair looks like it was combed with an electric eggbeater. Fiona breezes down the stairs.

LULU
(tired but happy to see her mom)
Good morning, Mom.

Fiona is fully dressed in fitted black pants, a loose white silk tank top, black pointy pumps, and her standard men's gold watch and diamond love bangles. She's wearing a pair of vintage Oliver Peoples sunglasses.

FIONA
(all business)
You're up early, Lulu.

LULU
I'm excited about the *Seas the Day* party tonight. Lex let me work on it. Mom, I wanna help you however I can.

Fiona lets her sunglasses slide down her nose. She looks at Lulu over the dark lenses.

FIONA
Lu, this party is not really a party. It's a way to thank my actors and crew for working so hard. And, most important, I've got Mr. Sanyo coming. Linc and I need to make him feel like a king, got it?

LULU
Got it.

FIONA
And, being British, I have no trouble showing respect for the king, especially one like Mr. Sanyo, who's already paid millions of dollars to let me make *Seas the Day*.

Linc bounds down the wide, floating staircase. He appears sporting dark sunglasses, slicked-back wet hair, expensive jeans that look battered, a James Perse black T-shirt, and Gucci flip-flops.

LINC
(calls from the middle of the stairs)

I'm not late yet!

Linc reaches the bottom and gives Lulu a quick kiss.

LINC

Lu, if I were you, I'd still be in bed.

LULU

I want to know if there's anything you guys want me to do for the party tonight.

Fiona crouches down in front of her daughter and flicks her sunglasses to the top of her head.

FIONA

Please, darling. No mischief tonight.

LINC
(looks at Lulu from above Fiona's head)

That means, specifically: lock up your insane dog and don't go near any of the food.

Alexis, in polka-dot pajama bottoms and a gray tank top, perches at the top of the stairs. Her long, mussed ponytail is the first clue that she's just rolled out of bed. She giggles.

175

> **LULU**
>
> I understand. All Mom's hard-working actors and crew have a super fun time and Mr. Sanyo has so much fun he gives Mom more money.

Linc winks. Fiona stands up.

> **LULU**
>
> My Ohana friends will come dressed and ready to perform and then watch the fireworks with me. We won't even talk to other guests. Right, Lex?

Lulu looks up at her sister.

Almost at the front door, Fiona pauses and shoots Alexis a "what's this?" look.

> **ALEXIS**
>
> Don't worry, Fiona, it'll be fine. They won't be performing their *Hilarious Hula.* Some of Lulu's camp pals are *très* talented.

Fiona and Linc EXIT.

INT. HARRISON ENTRANCE—CONTINUOUS

Lulu leaps from the chair and knocks over a mahogany bowl filled with kiwi. The brown fuzzy balls roll everywhere. Lulu tries to catch them but immediately steps on one and squishes it into the floor.

Maya comes into the entrance.

> MAYA

Lulu, this reminds me.

> LULU

Maya, I'm sorry. I'll clean up.

Maya takes Lulu's hand and leads her to the stairs.

> MAYA

I put a new pair of shoes in your room for you.

> LULU

For tonight? Party shoes?

> MAYA

Well, let's say they're for everything.

Lulu races up stairs, ducks into her room, and, after a minute, reappears. She holds toddler-sized cream-colored cut-out Mary Janes with orange floral straps.

> LULU

You mean these?

Maya's face folds in the usual worn lines as she smiles.

Lulu plows down the stairs and plunks down on the bottom one.

> LULU

These won't fit me.

MAYA

Right. They are for little ones when they first learn to walk, but I want you to have them.

Maya sits down next to Lulu. Lulu burrows her head into Maya's arm.

LULU
(muffled)

Why?

MAYA

Because I want you to slow down. Squeaky shoes make a child think about every step she takes. She takes a step. She hears squeak. Makes every step important. She can hear when she slows down or when she speeds up.

LULU

What if, sometimes, the kid doesn't even know what direction to walk?

Maya puts her arm around Lulu. Maya squeezes the tip of the shoe. The SQUEEEAK makes Lulu smile.

MAYA

Then that kid should take a moment to sit quietly.

SCENE 19: WHEN IT RAINS, IT POURS

INT./EXT. HARRISONS' HOUSE—SATURDAY NIGHT

INTERIOR SHOT—Camera pans to a tent full of handsome, fit men and beautiful, slim women. Waiters in Hawaiian shirts pass asparagus wrapped with ham and tofu balls. Fiona, in a long floral-printed wrap dress and spiky heels, floats among party guests. Linc wears his usual slouchy designer jeans with a Turnbull & Asser dress shirt, untucked. He drifts around the tent, slapping guys on the back and hugging women.

Lulu and Alexis poke their heads into the tent. Lulu wears her trademark orange skirt and a clean SURF MOLOKAI T-shirt. For the occasion, her hair has been somewhat tamed into a ponytail that looks like a pom-pom. Alexis wears skintight white jeans and a silver sheath tunic.

> LULU
> It's going great! And geez peas! The rain's stopped.

Lulu and Alexis both glance up. The gray sky is fading from purple to black. Stars can't be seen but neither can rain clouds or lightning.

> ALEXIS
> Not exactly great because I still don't see Mr. Sanyo.

LULU
(heading toward the house)
Let's check if he's inside.

Alexis teeters after her sister. Normally perfectly graceful on her heels, Alexis slips a bit on the wet *lanai*. She looks around embarrassed. Fortunately, no one notices.

INT. HARRISONS' KITCHEN—FIVE MINUTES LATER

Lulu and Alexis sneak into the kitchen. WAITERS bustle in and out.

ALEXIS
Seriously, I wonder why Sanyo hasn't showed.

Lulu leans over the counter.

LULU
Is this a chocolate lava cake?

She drags her finger around edge, then sticks it in her mouth.

ALEXIS
Lu! That's disgusting.

Lulu sucks the sweet, sticky chocolate off her finger.

Mr. Sanyo enters kitchen.

MR. SANYO
(booming voice)
Excuse me? Can someone store this for me?
(holds out a jar of peanut butter)
I add this to food for flavor, and this is the only brand
I'll use.

Everyone freezes. Lulu, however, bounces over and takes the jar.

LULU

Sure, I love PB—

CRASH. The glass jar shatters on the kitchen floor. It slid through Lulu's saliva-wet fingers.

LULU

I'm sooo sorry. I have another jar here I can share with you.

Mr. Sanyo gives Lulu a hard stare and leaves the kitchen.

EXT. *LANAI* and POOL AREA—THIRTY MINUTES LATER

Guests huddle in near darkness. Lights from inside the house cast shadows on the *lanai*. Small tea-light candles illuminate a path from the *lanai* to the stage floating in the pool.

LULU
(to Fiona and Linc)
How was I supposed to know that the solar lights needed a whole day of sunlight?

LINC
(not at all laid-back and cool)
Why'd YOU even have a say in the lights for this party?

FIONA
(a take-charge calm in her voice)
Forget it. The show must go on!

ALEXIS
Besides, it does look *très* romantic and dramatic.

All the Harrisons look toward the floating stage and the candlelight reflecting in the water around it.

Fiona and Linc walk to the far side of the pool and take the stage.

WIDE SHOT of Fiona and Linc standing in the middle of the floating stage. They look magical in the glimmer of the small candles. Fiona's dress shimmers from the bottom up.

FIONA
I want to thank you all very much for coming by our house tonight.

LINC
(grabbing a microphone from his wife)
And next time, let us know you're coming and we'll turn the lights on!

LAUGHING heard from the guests.

FIONA

I don't want to take much time for speeches. This night
is about us finally taking a few moments to relax. We've
all been working incredibly long hours.

Lulu, sitting at the edge of the pool, hears a commotion behind
her. She turns to see her Ohana pals. Auntie Moana corrals kids
in the living room. Lulu stands.

FIONA

There is only one person I'd like to have come up, so I can
thank him in front of all of you, and that's Mr. Hiyra Sanyo,
(CLAPPING) president of Sanyo Studios, who believed in
me and in *Seas the Day* becoming a great motion pic—

Lulu takes off toward her friends but keeps turning back to look
at her mother.

THUD. THWACK. Mr. Sanyo, in the darkness, BUMPS into
Lulu. They both SLIP on the rain-soaked floor. SPLASH. Mr.
Sanyo ends up in the pool. Not a sound can be heard except Mr.
Sanyo sputtering in the water.

Mr. Sanyo, not a good swimmer, and disoriented by the fall and
the darkness, struggles in the water. Lulu, Linc, and Fiona all
dive in.

LULU

I'm coming Mr.—

Linc beats Lulu. He smoothly and athletically brings Mr. Sanyo to the side of the pool.

LULU

I'm really—

Alexis appears with towels.

FIONA
(hisses from the pool)
Alexis, get the fireworks going. Distract everyone. NOW!

Alexis kicks off her shoes and dashes to find one of the Pele guys. Meanwhile, the Ohana kids pile onto the *lanai* to see what's happening.

Lulu, wrapped in a towel, squishes toward her friends.

LULU
Geez peas! I almost drowned the head of Mom's studio.

KENNA
That guy could barely doggie-paddle.

KAPONO
That guy's a worse swimmer than Watson.

Ohana kids laugh.

NOELANI
(softly)
Lu, it wasn't your fault.

184

LULU
(squinting in the darkness)
Hey! Noelani! What are you doing here?! You're supposed to be talking to your mom on her ship.

Noelani is dressed in the most beautiful deep-green ti-leaf hula skirt and wears a yellow hibiscus in her hair.

NOELANI
(whispers)
I'm gonna do it, Lu. Don't worry. I can hula tonight. My mom understands I'm doing this for you and...for me.

FAAAROOOMPH! CRAAAACK! PAAAACHOOOOM!

A screaming firework flies up. It shoots toward the night sky, but jerks down and lands near guests huddled on the *lanai*.

A second firework takes off and fizzles out just above the party tent.

The third explosive smacks into bamboo hedges next to the house. Stalks begin to smolder.

GUESTS and WAITERS
FIRE!!

CAMERA PANS the scene. Alexis and Maxwell run into the house hand in hand. Cast and crew members scramble inside and then out the front door.

Auntie Moana gathers up the Ohana kids and calmly leads

them to the beach at the edge of the Harrison's backyard. Uncle Akamu dashes toward the burning, crackling bamboo. He grabs towels from the damp ground and starts whacking yellow-white flames. Lulu approaches and gives him her wet towels. Since everything is damp from rain, the fire begins to sputter out.

UNCLE AKAMU
Mahalo, Lulu. Now get away from here.

LULU
Considering how many people here want to kill me right now, I think I'm safest by the fire.

ACT III: A HAPPY LANDING

SCENE 1: THE DAWN'S EARLY LIGHT

EXT. INFINITY POOL—SUNDAY, 7 A.M.

 CUT!! I have NO idea how I'm gonna get through this day. Anyway, to sum up last night, my parents are furious. Mr. Sanyo is furious. Getting in his car, he told Mom that Sanyo Studios is done with her! Of course, he was saying this while he was dripping wet and couldn't see because his glasses were somewhere at the bottom of our pool, so I'm secretly hoping he didn't really mean it. Rather than helping Mom and Dad, and supporting them as a family member should, I turned everything into a mess that I can't see a way to fix. But first things first. I need to apologize *pronto*. OK, return to: ACTION!!

Birds sing. Soft orangey light slowly glows over the gentle, purple sky. Linc swims laps across the long pool. He's like a machine, rarely taking a breath and never stopping.

> LULU
> (loudly)

Dad!

Linc doesn't hear. His head isn't above water long enough.

> LULU
> (hollers)

Daaad!

Linc, without breaking his stroke, gives Lulu a wave.

> LULU

I want to apologize.

Lulu, still in pajamas, comes to the pool's edge. She holds two glasses full of white, creamy drinks.

> LULU

I've made us coconut smoothies...to ask for your forgiveness.

Without slowing, Linc flashes five fingers.

Unsure if that means five laps, five seconds, or five minutes, Lulu squats at pools edge.

> LULU

Daaahhhh...

SPLLLLLAAAASH!!

Lulu and two thick drinks tumble into the crystal-clear pool.

Linc speeds over to her.

Lulu bubbles to the surface. Coconut chunks cling to her hair. She swims to the side. Linc pulls out the two glasses and sets them on the pool's edge.

LINC
(grinning)
I think this pool is a hazard, babe. We should probably fill it in.

LULU
(struggles to look her dad in the eye)
Dad, I've made a mess.

Linc flips his swimming goggles to the top of his head.

LINC
(chuckles)
Yes, you have. My pool water's a little murky and so is my movie career.

Lulu notices a cloud-shaped smoothie floating on the water toward them. She shakes her head.

LULU
So you're not too mad at me? You're not going to send me to Timbuktu or something?

LINC
(more serious tone)
Not Timbuktu. But L.A. maybe.

Linc ducks his head underwater to slick back his thick hair.
(now above the surface)
Fiona and I have to figure out what to do. Your mom will
have way more free time after today.

CAMERA FOCUSES ON FIONA. She stands regally a few
feet from the pool.

FIONA
(sharp tone)
C'mon, Linc! We need to get to the set. I have to reshoot
scenes you messed up yesterday.

Fiona is fully dressed in billowing navy pants and a crisp,
white blouse. A blue-and-white-striped silky sweater is draped
around her narrow shoulders. Huge sunglasses cover the top
half of her face.

LINC
(hard tone)
You're not going to be my boss for too much longer. Let
me relax.

FIONA
(cold and stiff)
You can relax when the NEW director takes over.

190

Linc jumps out of the pool and grabs his towel. Lulu remains in the water.

FIONA

As for you, Lulu...

LULU

Mom, I got up super-looper early to say I was sorry for everything. I...

FIONA
(staring down at Lulu through her sunglasses)
Seas the Day is over for me. Last night, Mr. Sanyo fired me. Sanyo Studios is hiring a new director.

Lulu looks up at her mother from the pool.

LULU

Mom, I only—

FIONA

It's time I sent you home.

Lulu ducks underwater so her tears mingle with the smoothie-infused pool water. After a few seconds, she comes to the surface.

LULU

Mom? If you're not working on the movie for the rest of the summer, then maybe we can just explore O'ahu together. Find old koa trees? See monk seals at the Honolulu Aquarium? Visit the—

FIONA

For your information, in 1778, Captain James Cook, a British citizen, like me, was the first European to discover the Hawaiian Islands. But guess what he did?

LULU

What?

FIONA

He actually sailed past O'ahu and landed on Kauai. So that's what I'm going to do. Of course, I should have never first landed on O'ahu, but now I'm going to close down everything here and go off to Kauai for a few weeks.

LULU

Mom, can't we all go? That sounds like a real summer vacation.

FIONA

I told you weeks ago. I canceled summer vacation!

 CUT!! This is one of those times I've gotta tell you how I feel inside: miserable. I know scripts are supposed to only show, but showing how I feel now would have me drench my mother with pool water and then do somersaults underwater till she changes her mind. Back to: ACTION!!

SCENE 2: BIKINI BRAIN FREEZE

INT. ALEXIS'S ROOM—SUNDAY, 9 A.M.

Mini-mountains of bikinis have sprung up all around Alexis's normally tidy room. Tops and bottoms are piled by color and style. The highest mountain, so far, is red tops.

Lulu enters after a quick knock. If she waits for an answer, she knows she'd be told "go away."

> LULU
> (glancing around)
> Geez peas! You've got a lot of bikinis.

Alexis ignores her and continues opening drawers, dumping out every bikini inside, and slamming the drawers shut. Then she sorts and stacks bikini tops and bottoms.

> LULU
> What are you doing? Are you having a bikini garage sale with all these?

Lulu carefully makes her way around hills of yellow tops and lavender bottoms toward Alexis's puffy, white, unmade bed. Lulu accidentally stumbles on flower-print bottoms. They scatter under the bed.

> ALEXIS
> Lulu, just get out! I've got lots going on here.

LULU

I can see that. You've got a mess-a-rama in here.

ALEXIS

(waves her bony wrist around)
It's not as bad as the mess we made out there last night.

Lulu crawls under the bed and fishes out three skimpy, flowered bottoms.

LULU

It's really clean under your bed.

ALEXIS

(tugs nervously at the ends of her hair)
Good, because I'm thinking of hiding under there till Fiona ships us home. Or maybe I should try swimming to L.A. this afternoon. I wish I knew how far it was.

LULU

It's about two thousand five hundred and fifty miles. More than you could swim in a day, plus you'd have to deal with rip currents, trade winds, rough seas, carnivorous marine life, and—

ALEXIS

That all sounds better than facing Fiona. Not to mention Maxwell.

LULU

Well, I came in here to figure out how we can get Mom
hired back to finish the end of the movie.

ALEXIS

What are you talking about? *Seas the Day* will have a new
director to finish the movie and shoot the big final scene. And,
even worse for Fiona, Linc will be working for the new director.

Alexis pauses to toss a black top on the black-bikini-top mound.

ALEXIS

This family has been busted up for the rest of summer.

LULU

That's exactly why we need to combine our brains and
figure out how to weave us all back together.

ALEXIS

Do you have island fever or something? You trying to
help might be the single worst thing that happened to
this family all summer. The second would be my agreeing
to do anything with you.

Alexis pulls out a whole drawer and dumps more trendy bikini
pieces on the bed. She starts separating tops from bottoms. Lulu
spots an orange bikini in Alexis's new pile.

LULU
(points to it)
You have a bikini in my favorite color?

ALEXIS
(plucks out the suit)
The color of this bikini is called cantaloupe. If I give this to you, will you get out of my room? I'm dealing with a bikini brain freeze!

Alexis tosses the suit toward Lulu.

LULU
What's a "bikini brain freeze"?

Alexis, eyes bulging, sits down on a mound of white bikini bottoms. She draws her knees up to her body and hugs them. She drops her head so her forehead rests on the tops of her knees.

LULU
Are you sick right now from the bikini-brain-freeze thing?

ALEXIS
(lifts her head)
Right now...
(now screaming)
I'm SICK of YOU!

Lulu squeezes her eyes shut.

LULU
I thought we—

ALEXIS

Don't finish any sentence that has the word "*we*" in it. Thanks to you, Maxwell thinks I'm an idiot. Linc and Fiona won't have a movie. And now I'm trapped on an island in the worst summer ever!

LULU

—were a team.

Alexis stands up and gets back to sorting bikinis.

ALEXIS

Well, you've been dropped, traded, fired. Don't talk to me until sometime around Christmas.

Lulu slowly heads toward the door.

LULU

What's bikini brain freeze anyway?

ALEXIS

It's that I can't think about anything except counting and organizing my swimsuits. OK?! It's calming me down. At least, it was working before you came in. NOW GET OUT.

SCENE 3: L.A. CALLING

INT. LULU'S BEDROOM—SUNDAY, 10 A.M.

Lulu lies on the floor of her room, stacking coral. Since the white, hard chunks have textured surfaces and curved edges, Lulu can't get more than three pieces on top of each other before they clatter down.

DO-DO-DO-DO-DO-DOOO-DO-DO-DO-DO-DOOOO.

Hawaii Five-O theme music muffles from somewhere in Lulu's closet. She rifles through skirts, surf T-shirts, and checkered Vans on the closet floor.

LULU
(to herself)

Please be my Ohana friends wanting to know if I'm still alive. *Kokoa*, please.

She finds her phone in a shoe. She punches the screen with her forefinger.

(almost breathless)

Aloha, it's me, Lulu.

Lulu leans back on the floor of her closet.

GIRL'S VOICE THROUGH THE PHONE

Surprise! Lu?

LULU
(checks the number on the phone screen)

Hey? This is a number from Los Angeles! Sophia? You're calling?

SOPHIA
(warm, sweet voice)

It's me.

Lulu can tell that her best friend from home is smiling. She can feel the smile coming through the phone and breaks into a grin of her own as she leans against the closet door.

SOPHIA

Thank you for sending me the video of the Halona Blowhole.

LULU

It's awesome, right? How the water shoots up?

SOPHIA

Loved it. And, well, everyone here keeps watching *Hilarious Hula*.

Lulu's smile disappears. She tilts her head back.

LULU
(sad)

That seems SO long ago.

SOPHIA
(serious)

I sure miss you, Lulu.

LULU

I feel lost, Soph, and I don't know that I've ever felt like this before.

PAUSE. Sound of SLUSHING water.

SOPHIA

What's that noise? Is it raining there?

Lulu listens.

LULU

That's just Watson drinking out of the toilet bowl.
(chuckles)
He's only been drinking toilet water in Hawaii. I think
it's because toilet water stays cooler than the water in
his bowl. It's so HOT here!

SOPHIA

Hotter than L.A.?

LULU

Different hot.
(pauses)
But I think I'll be back in L.A. hot soon.

SOPHIA

That's why I'm calling.
(voice drops)
Lu, I heard from my mom that your mom isn't finishing
her movie.

LULU
(quietly)
It's my fault. I...had this idea that family was about
supporting each other.

200

SOPHIA

It is.

LULU

Well, not MY family. You don't even want to know what happened, but let's just say me trying to help got ambulances and fire trucks involved.

SILENCE.

LULU
(soft, sad voice)
I ruined my parents' movie. And I ruined spending summer as a family.

SOPHIA

Lu, sometimes parents just have to put work first.

Lulu plunks down on her messy closet floor.

SQUEEEEEAAAAK. Lulu lifts her bottom and tosses a squeaky shoe into a corner.

LULU

Well, what's so great about family stuff? I shouldn't have even cared about my parents being with me. That's so babyish anyway.

Watson wanders over to Lulu. He licks her face.

Lulu can't help giggling.

SOPHIA

Well, at least you're laughing about it.

LULU

No! I'm laughing because Watson's kissing my face.

SOPHIA

That's gross if his muzzle was in the toilet.

LULU

He was just lapping the water, not licking the toilet bowl.

SOPHIA

(chuckles)

Lu, only you wouldn't mind getting smooched by a dog's toilet tongue. Which proves, you're the same old Lulu. So, listen: You're still in Honolulu! Find monk seals, snorkel reefs, touch real koa trees, and eat more yummy stuff. Send me more pictures and videos!

LULU

Thanks, Soph. But all my camp friends, who I did that stuff with, are probably never talking to me again.

SOPHIA

Hey, if they're really friends, then they're probably home wondering why you're not talking to them.

Lulu takes a deep breath.

LULU

I'll try them 'cause my family doesn't care about me and I don't care anymore about them.

SOPHIA
(softly)

Lu, you love your family. Don't start thinking that's not important.

LULU

Aloha, Soph, and *mahalo*. I love that you called me.

Lulu clicks off and stretches out her legs.

SQUEEEEAAAAK.

LULU

Those silly baby shoes. Can't I move in this closet without squeaking?

Lulu picks one up, squeezes it zillions of times, and realizes... she's got to think carefully about each next step.

SCENE 4: MOCHI MIRACLE

INT. BUBBIES ICE CREAM SHOP—SUNDAY, 11 A.M.

Bubbies Hand Made Ice Cream and Desserts looks like an old-fashioned ice cream parlor from any American town except for a small blackboard that lists the daily *mochi* flavors.

CUT!! In case you don't know what *mochi* is, it's one of the most best desserts ever, and coming from me, a dessert expert, you know that it's gotta be amazing! *Mochi* starts with ice cream of any flavor. The ice cream gets wrapped in a gummy, sweet outside that's made from pounded sticky white rice. Oh, just so you know, at Bubbies, you can get your *mochi* dipped in chocolate. OK, back to, ACTION!!

Lulu and Maya wait in a long line. Lulu stares at the homemade ice creams in the bright, icy case.

                    MAYA
How about you try something new? Like one of those sundaes?

Maya points to a menu hanging behind the counter.

                    LULU
Nope! I'm here to get my most favorite fave.

              MAYA and LULU
                  (together)
Chocolate peanut butter *mochi*.

                    LULU
                  (smiles)
Dipped in chocolate.

Lulu and Maya scooch closer to the register. The line moves slowly.

LULU
(rests her head on Maya's arm)
I've gotta figure out how to get my mom's job back, so she can direct *Seas the Day* to the end. (pause) But don't worry, I'm not rushing into anything.

Lulu reaches into her tote bag and pulls out a squeaky Mary Jane.

Maya puts her arm around Lulu's shoulders.

Lulu and Maya slide up. Lulu glances over and notices the flaming red hair and the gigantic belly.

LULU

Mrs. Adams?

Mrs. Adams grins. Her rosy, plump cheeks rise on her pretty round face.

LULU
(talking speedy)
Aloha! It's me, Lulu! Ya know, your husband saved my puggie from drowning.

MRS. ADAMS
(eyes twinkling)
That was your dog? Well, my husband hasn't taken that goofy ALOHA hat off his head.

MAYA
(glancing at Mrs. Adams's tummy)

Looks like that baby could be coming any day.

MRS. ADAMS
(leans in to Lulu and Maya)
She could be born right here at Bubbies!

Lulu's eyes bulge. Mrs. Adams winks.

MRS. ADAMS
I'm kidding. But it's so close now that I told Colonel Adams he better cut it with working ALL the time.

LULU
That's super-looper of you. My mom and dad work all the time.

MRS. ADAMS
(looks into Lulu's eyes)
Lots do. Actually,
(pauses and leans even closer to Lulu)
Noelani's mom is coming home. Colonel Adams is bringing her back to Honolulu to take over command from him before our baby is born.

LULU
(eyes bulge even bigger than before)
Geez peas! When?

Maya edges Lulu forward.

MRS. ADAMS
As soon as Marine command arranges her transport from her ship.

(rubs her belly)
This baby isn't going to wait too much longer!

SCENE 5: MYSTERY MOCHI MAN

INT./EXT. BUBBIES—CONTINUOUS

MAN BEHIND THE COUNTER
May I help you?

The man looks exhausted. His name tag, that says MILO, sags on his shirt.

LULU
May I please have four chocolate peanut butter *mochi* dipped in chocolate? For here.

MILO
No.

Lulu smiles at him. She thinks he's kidding.

MILO
No really. You can't. Someone called from his car, and we had to do a huge order of chocolate peanut butter *mochi*. He wanted three dozen.

                    LULU
How could you sell him ALL of them?

                    MILO
                 (whispering)
He's, like, important. He makes movies.

                    LULU
But...

                    MILO
                 (to Lulu)
Look, kiddo, how about some exotic *mochi* today. Like
lychee or guava or passion fruit or....

                    LULU
Or I can help you carry out the order. You need an
extra hand?

Milo looks behind him and sees his coworker juggling six
wobbling boxes.

                    MILO
Sure that might be helpful. Then I'll give you free *mochi*,
any other flavor, when you come back in. You won't have
to wait in line.

Lulu scoots behind the counter. A WORKER hands her three
boxes and then motions for her to follow him outside. Lulu
tries to hold the boxes in a neat stack, but the *mochi* roll around,

making the boxes feels like something's alive inside. She clutches the bottom box and rests her chin on the top one.

EXT. BUBBIES ICE CREAM SHOP—CONTINUOUS

They round the corner of Bubbies and enter a small driveway. A long white limo idles. When the DRIVER sees the employee with the boxes, he opens the front passenger door. The employee puts his boxes in first.

> LULU
> (to the driver)
> If I move my chin, I think they'll all fall. Can ya grab the boxes?

The driver takes the boxes and in a flash Lulu knocks on the rear passenger window. The thick, dark glass smoothly slides down.

Lulu comes face-to-face with Mr. Sanyo!

> LULU
> (speaks extra speedy)
> *Aloha!* It's me, Lulu Harrison.

Mr. Sanyo runs his freshly buffed fingernails through his neatly combed hair. His mirrored sunglasses reflect Lulu to Lulu.

> MR. SANYO
> (no humor in his voice)
> I can see that. Don't come too close to me. I don't want to get wet or damaged somehow.

LULU
(speaking super-fast)
Sorry to bother you. I was curious who ordered all the chocolate peanut butter *mochi*. Now Bubbies is out. That's OK 'cause maybe I can come back tomorrow. I really just wanted to know who else loved chocolate peanut butter as much as I do.

A wind comes up and blows Lulu's wild hair. Clumps land in her mouth, and she pulls them out.

Mr. Sanyo's driver approaches to shoo Lulu away. Mr. Sanyo waves him off.

MR. SANYO
(still in mirrored sunglasses)
You love chocolate peanut butter *mochi* also?

LULU
(smiling)
It's one of the yummiest things to eat on O'ahu. And, trust me, I've sampled lots of runner-ups.

MR. SANYO
It's the perfect combination—of American and Japanese. *Mochi*, the Japanese treat I ate since I was a boy, filled with peanut butter ice cream that can only be found in America.
(pauses)
Why don't you have one of my *mochi*? Actually, take one of the boxes.
(he gives a tiny smile)

Bring it home to your mother. Tell her I'm sorry that my studio can't back her directing the movie anymore.

LULU

But why not?

The Driver approaches to give Lulu a yank. Mr. Sanyo puts up his smooth hand to hold him off another moment.

MR. SANYO

I don't expect you to understand this, but I'll tell you.
(he slides his window all the way down)
Seas the Day has taken TOO long to make and, therefore, is costing TOO much money. Additionally, the picture remains absent of its final military scene.

 CUT!! This is one more of those times that I have to tell you what's going on inside me. The camera on the outside would show me totally not moving, like, not even twitching. But my brain is spinning. I'm mashing together a plan. And I'm summoning up my inner *koa*, ya know, bravery, to pull it off. At this second, I am absolutely convinced of one thing: *mochi* might be magic. OK, back to: ACTION!!

LULU

Well, actually, Mr. Sanyo, sir, that landing scene is pretty much all put together. My mother has been working secretly with U.S. Marines Corps Forces Command all summer.

Mr. Sanyo opens his door and steps his tall, lean frame out of the car. There's not a wrinkle in his dark blue suit.

LULU
(whispering)
It all had to be arranged in a hush-hush way. And the military will only give this opportunity to my mom. She's the one who's been, ummm, given the top-secret information.

MR. SANYO
(pulls off his mirrored glasses)
Top secret?

LULU
(talks super fast)
But super geez please, Mr. Sanyo. Don't tell anyone.

MR. SANYO
When is this supposed to be happening?

LULU
Ummm, how long are you going to be in Honolulu?

MR. SANYO
(eyes sparkle with interest)
That depends. I fly on my own plane, so it takes off whenever I need it to.

Mr. Sanyo gets back into his car but the car door remains open.

LULU
Well, my sister, Alexis, will call your assistant, as soon as the top-secret filming information is, ahhh, ahhh, available.

Mr. Sanyo leans toward Lulu.

MR. SANYO
(lowers his voice)
If it's confidential, have her call me directly.

Mr. Sanyo hands Lulu his thick, white card with his private cell phone. The Driver shuts Mr. Sanyo's door.

LULU
(trying to sound casual to the driver)
Can you give me that box of peanut butter chocolate *mochi* Mr. Sanyo said I could have?

While he retrieves the *mochi*, Lulu whistles "Yankee Doodle." Concentrating on the song slows down the flip-flopping in her stomach.

SCENE 6: GETTING THE HOUSE IN ORDER

EXT. NOELANI'S HOUSE—FIFTEEN MINUTES LATER

The Watson Wagon pulls into the driveway. Lulu races out of the car and jogs across the small lawn. She notices that the American flag flies next to the front door.

> LULU

NOE!! It's me, Lulu. You home?

Lulu pushes open the front door.

INT. NOELANI'S LIVING ROOM—CONTINUOUS

Noelani vacuums. Tutu is on a chair, wiping down windows. Lulu waves to get their attention.

> LULU

I heard your mom's coming home! How soon?

> NOELANI
> (a smile creeping across her face)

I know.
> (pauses)

But I don't know when.

Lulu hugs her friend. Watson runs in with James following behind.

> LULU

Is she coming home today?

> NOELANI
> (murmurs)

We missed, ummm, talking to her last night.

> LULU
> (quietly)

That would be my fault.

Noelani smiles at her friend.

NOELANI
No, it's NOT. Besides, Tutu got a call from the Marine command office saying Mom's on her way.

TUTU
They said she's coming in on a special transport. It's all very rush and hush.

Watson rolls over the carpet where Noelani has just vacuumed.

LULU
How do we find out?

NOELANI
We just wait.

Tutu steps down from the chair. James takes her hand and helps her.

TUTU
Why do you need to know, Lulu? You'll meet Noelani's mother soon enough.

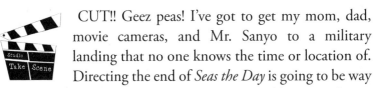 CUT!! Geez peas! I've got to get my mom, dad, movie cameras, and Mr. Sanyo to a military landing that no one knows the time or location of. Directing the end of *Seas the Day* is going to be way harder than I thought. Since every minute could count, I better get back to: ACTION!!

LULU

I came rushing over here because we have to plan for both our mothers.

NOELANI

What do you mean?

LULU

Your mom deserves a big Welcome Home! Ya know, music. Food. A banner. Entertainment. People cheering. The works. Maybe even TV stations!

NOELANI

I don't think we have time.

LULU

Sure we do!

NOELANI

And doing a party like that, we'd need lots of people to help.

LULU

No problem!

NOELANI

What you're describing sounds like it's from a movie.

LULU

Well, for better or worse, and lately it's been for worse, that's my world. So, let's do a Hollywood Homecoming for Lieutenant Colonel Nui!

Noelani sinks into the cushy couch and pulls herself into a ball.

NOELANI
(whispering)
I don't like to be near all that attention. A quiet thing
is better.

Tutu and James, who have been joking and laughing, now
break off.

TUTU
That's a wonderful idea. I've never done a party like
that. And since it's MY daughter coming home, I say,
"Lulu, roll 'em!"

NOELANI
Wait. What are we planning for your mom?

LULU
To get her job back!

SCENE 7: TEAMING UP

INT. SPLASH! BATHING SUIT SHOP—THIRTY MINUTES LATER

Alexis strolls around the store, checking out all colors, shapes,
and sizes of bikinis. Once in a while she pulls a hanger from the
rack but soon clanks it back.

ALEXIS
(bored tone)
Shawna, isn't there anything new since last time I was here?

Shawna sits on a stool behind the register.

SHAWNA
Lex, you were just here two days ago.

Lulu, followed by Noelani and Watson pulling James, tumbles into Splash! They are giddy with nerves and excitement. One withering look from Alexis, however, hushes them.

ALEXIS
(to her sister)
There's not one reason I can think of that you're here. It's NOT Christmas. I'm off from you for a couple more seasons, at least. You've caused me enough humiliations for one lifetime, let alone one summer.

LULU
Lex, I figured out how to get Mom rehired to direct *Seas the Day!*

ALEXIS
And I've figured out that one more scheme of yours could cause Fiona to have a gigantic volcanic eruption the likes of which the Hawaiian Islands have never seen.

LULU

Which is why I need you, Lex.

ALEXIS

Which is why I need to stay away from you, Lulu.

Noelani slinks behind a rack of sunglasses.

JAMES

Ahh-humm. Pardon me, ladies. Watson and I are going to duck out to look for something to eat.

LULU

No, wait here.

Lulu fishes around in her I USED TO BE A PLASTIC BOTTLE bag and pulls out a *li hing mui* butterfly-shaped lollipop. She waves it in Watson's direction. He trots over.

SHAWNA

Wait. Your pug eats lollipops?

LULU

Sure. He and I usually share a few a day. And look what else I found.

Pulls out the orange bikini top Alexis had tossed her that morning.

LULU

Lex, will you help me put this on?

Lulu shakes the top over her head like it's a pom-pom.

ALEXIS

You'd put on a bikini? That's crazy.

LULU

I'd do something mega-looper crazy for you. Besides, most of my kid life, you've been telling me to wear bikinis.

Alexis's perfectly waxed eyebrows knit together.

ALEXIS

Lu, I admit, it might be impossible to find a bikini that works for you.

LULU

Then help me. 'Cause, Lex, we can pull off impossible things together.

Lulu shuffles through skimpy bottoms hanging nearby.

LULU

There's no better teammate than you but—

ALEXIS

No buts! You're right. For any tricky, delicate, or complicated assignment, you need *moi*.

A smile forms at the corners of Lulu's mouth.

NOELANI
(lightly clears her throat)
That's what Lulu always says, Alexis. That no one can do what you can do. You're the master of getting people to do what you want.

Alexis shakes her long, luxurious hair.

It's quiet in the store…except for the sound of Watson slobbering up the lollipop.

ALEXIS
I'm actually kinda bored bikini shopping. What's this about? You need me to film something like *Hilarious Hula*?

LULU
Not exactly. More like getting Mom to film the last scene of *Seas the Day*.

Alexis rolls her big violet eyes.

ALEXIS
Seriously? Lulu, you're not serious?

SHAWNA
Sounds exciting!

LULU
You're gonna have to get Mom, Dad, the rest of the crew, and Mr. Sanyo on location.

ALEXIS

You're nuts!

LULU

But we don't know the day or time or location quite yet.

NO RESPONSE.

Alexis sits down next to Watson.

ALEXIS

OK. I need a lick of the lollipop, Watson, because what I'm about to do is crazier than sharing a lollipop with a pug.

SCENE 8: PARTY MAKES PERFECT

EXT. AUNTIE MOANA AND UNCLE AKAMU'S HOUSE— SUNDAY, 1 P.M.

The Watson Wagon skids up to the modest house. Lulu races to the front door. Noelani and James follow. Watson leaps from the car and sniffs the ground.

LULU
(calls out)

Anyone home?

(panicky)
I don't see the blue van here.

The front door opens. Auntie Moana comes out a smile on her lips, but her eyes look puzzled.

AUNTIE MOANA
Aloha. I love seeing you, but there's no Ohana Camp on the weekends.

LULU
First, Auntie, I'm so sorry about last night.

Auntie sits down on a front porch step. She takes Lulu's hands in her own.

AUNTIE MOANA
No more of that. Everyone is fine.
(looks from Lulu to Noelani to James and Watson)
Now, what can I do for you today?

Noelani looks up from her toes.

NOELANI
(softly)
We're planning surprises for our moms.

Noelani hesitates.

LULU
(speedy)
Noelani's mom is coming home! We want to do a gigantic welcome-home party, but we need help.

Auntie Moana, usually calm and serene, leaps from the step.

AUNTIE MOANA
That's fantastic news! Let's get going.
(looks at Noelani)
When's she coming? Where should we surprise her?

Noelani, normally so shy and hoping to be invisible, answers.

NOELANI
I don't know.

AUNTIE MOANA
Don't know which?

PAUSE

LULU
We don't know anything. That's super-looper-dooper why we need help. We need to plan for this to happen anytime, anywhere.

It becomes quiet except for the singing of thrushes. FINALLY...

AUNTIE MOANA
Lulu, what are we doing for your mother?

Lulu shakes her head.

> LULU
>
> My mom? Let's just say I'm trying to surprise two moms with one stone.

SCENE 9: AKUA OF OHANA
(The Spirit of Family)

EXT. UNCLE AKAMU AND AUNTIE MOANA'S HOUSE—CONTINUOUS

> LULU
>
> Noelani, you need to think hula!

> NOELANI
>
> That's something I just can't think about.

> LULU
>
> There's something special inside you, Noe, and letting it out would be a great welcome-home present for your mom.

Noelani walks away from her friend. Before she disappears inside Auntie Moana's house, she turns back to Lulu.

> NOELANI
>
> *Mahalo*, Lulu. Even if I don't have *koa*, I'm really lucky to have you as my friend.

CUT!! The next hour is a total whirl. It shows exactly what *ohana* means! Family. Plain and simple. To act like family, people don't have to be related. The spirit of helping each other and doing things together swirls around families and friends alike. All my Hawaiian friends and people I didn't even know were friends totally came together to do something for Noelani that she couldn't ever ask for herself. And for me! Seems my pals don't want me shipped back to L.A. either. Since so many people do so much so fast, I'm going to show you what happens in one of those MONTAGES. So here goes. A series of brief shots of my pals getting a welcome-home party together for when and where they don't even know. OK. Back to: ACTION!!

MONTAGE—OHANA TEAM GOES INTO ACTION

★ Uncle Akamu and Caridyn stand onstage. A crowd dressed in Hawaiian shirts and dresses gathers to watch their hotel's *luau* performance. Auntie Moana walks onto the stage and whispers to Uncle Akamu and Caridyn. Uncle Akamu snaps his ukulele into its case. Caridyn swings her drum over her shoulder. All three wave and head for the nearest exit.

★ Khloe and the Cs sway and shuffle on a big stage with Island School of Hula girls. They're in yet another performance at the mall. Distracted by commotion, Khloe misses her arm movements. The commotion is Lulu and Alexis. They motion wildly for Khloe. She hops off the stage and soon motions for Cate and Carole to ditch the show and follow her.

★ Kenna and Kapono sit on a bench at an outdoor table. Kenna threads tuberose and orchids onto nylon string. Kapono pulls his sister's hair. Kenna shoves her brother off the bench. He gets up and helps Kenna string *leis*.

★ Liam and his mother knock on a door. Mrs. Lyons, Khloe's mother, opens it. They explain that they need her connections. Mrs. Lyons flashes a perfect toothy smile and nods.

★ Maleko walks down his driveway, carrying his surfboard. He puts it down to answer his cell phone. Within seconds, he runs into his house and races back out with his drums strapped to his back. He hops on his bike and rides away.

★ James, wearing his dog butler chauffeur cap, hacks away at long, sword-shaped ti leaves. Watson sleeps in the sunshine nearby.

★ Noelani stands by herself in front of a mirror in Uncle Akamu and Auntie Moana's house. Her legs slide and step. Her arms flow from side to side. She's practicing a beautiful hula, but every time noise is heard from anywhere in the house, she freezes.

BACK TO SCENE

EXT. AUNTIE MOANA AND UNCLE AKAMU'S BACKYARD—ONE HOUR LATER

Sounds of chatting and laughter can be heard. CAMERA PANS the backyard. Khloe and the Cs paint a banner. Liam and Maleko practice the ukulele and drum together. Auntie Moana and Maya roll *laulau* into taro leaves. Uncle Akamu and Caridyn hack open coconuts.

Noelani, however, sits alone at an outdoor table. One last slice of cold Hawaiian pizza sits on a paper plate in front of her. Lulu approaches.

> LULU
> "Welcome-Home Party Hollywood-style" is in the works!

> NOELANI
> (looks at her friend)
> We've got a little problem. We still don't know when or where my mom's coming home.

> LULU
> Not a little problem. And not one I haven't thought of. C'mon.

Noelani gets to her feet.

> NOELANI
> Where are we going?

> LULU
> We've got to go talk to the guy in charge.

SCENE 10: MILITARY TIME

EXT. GUARD POST, MARINE CORPS TRAINING AREA BELLOWS—EARLY AFTERNOON

The Watson Wagon pulls up in front of two SOLDIERS holding big guns. They stand in front of barbed wire and tall, closed gates.

Lulu jumps out first.

> LULU
> (brightly)
> Hi! We come in peace. Don't shoot!

> SERGEANT 1
> You'll have to move along, ma'am.

> LULU
> I'm here to see, ummm, Colonel Adams.

> SERGEANT 1
> (grabs a clipboard)
> Do you have an appointment?

Noelani remains seated in the car.

> LULU
> Ahhh. Not officially. See, I met him on the beach when he resc—

> SERGEANT 2
> That's where he is again today. Marines have been out there practicing landings all morning.

SERGEANT 1
(to Sergeant 2)
Hey, man, that information was classified. What's wrong with you?
(to Lulu)
Look, ma'am, the beach is now open. Just head down the road.

Watson, in his "LARGE AND IN CHARGE" shirt, waddles over to Lulu

BEEP BEEP!

A car horn TOOTS from inside the gate.

Mrs. Adams, her red hair like a swarm around her smiling face, waves out the window.

SERGEANT 1
(to woman in the car)
Mrs. Adams, you'll have to wait a moment. We have a situation here.

MRS. ADAMS
(trying to hide a chuckle)
A situation?

SERGEANT 1
Yes, ma'am. Concerning your husband.

MRS. ADAMS
(chuckle escapes)
Really? A situation with a chubby pug and an excited
little girl?

SERGEANT 2
Yes, ma'am.

MRS. ADAMS
Well, I have a situation myself.

Mrs. Adams exits her car, walks through a side gate, and comes toward Lulu and James. Actually, she waddles as noticeably as Watson. Her hands are around her belly.

MRS. ADAMS
(to Sergeant 2)
I'll take it from here.
(to Lulu)
Hey! Is that you, Lulu?

Lulu wipes her forehead with the back of her hand. Without her ALOHA cap, Lulu has to lather her face with thick, white sunscreen. The goop makes her forehead sweaty.

LULU
Aloha, Mrs. Adams. Am I glad to see you!

MRS. ADAMS
That must be the pug Colonel Adams fished *ooooouuuuch*
out of the water.

Mrs. Adams' face twists. It's clear she had a pang of pain. Lulu and James rush toward her.

> LULU

Are you OK?

> MRS. ADAMS
> (waves them off)

Yes. Are you OK? What are you doing here?

> LULU
> (looks toward the car again)

Well, it's Noelani. We're trying to find out when her mom might be coming back—and where.

> MRS. ADAMS

Lieutenant Colonel Nui? It better be soon because this baby is coming. That was our deal. I told Colonel Adams he better take leave and turn over command by the time this baby is born. And he's running *ooooouch* out of time.

> LULU

You better get to the hospital or something. I don't think you're OK.

> MRS. ADAMS

I'm fine. But I might kill Colonel Adams. He's still hanging *ooooouch* out at the beach somewhere.

JAMES
(bowing slightly)
Madam, allow me to take you to the hospital. Let's get
you off your feet.

James puts his arm around Mrs. Adams and walks her to the
Watson Wagon.

James makes Mrs. Adams comfortable in the Watson Wagon.
He tosses out Lulu's bag, and Watson's leash and sunglasses to
allow Mrs. Adams to lie down.

MRS. ADAMS
(smiling)
To the hospital!

JAMES
Yes, ma'am!

MRS. ADAMS
(to Lulu)
Will you find my husband and tell him to get Noelani's
mother here noooooow and toooooooo...
(her face twitches in pain)
...get himself to the hospital! ON THE DOUBLE!!

LULU
Yes! Mrs. Adams, count on me.

> **NOELANI**
> (small voice)

And me too.

Noelani had quietly gotten out of the car and come around to see Mrs. Adams off.

> **MRS. ADAMS**
> (a soft, warm voice)
> Oh, your poor mother! Having been away all those months and missing her daughter!
> (closes her eyes and takes some deep breaths)
> She's supposed to land at Kaneohe at sixteen hundred, but that's going to be tooooo late.

James nudges Lulu and Noelani away so he can shut the door.

> **JAMES**
> Girls, I'm on an important mission.

He gives them a little mock salute.

> **LULU**
> (eyes wide)
> Wait! James, do you speak military? What's 1600 hours?

James dives into the driver's seat and turns on the engine.

> **JAMES**
> I speak pooch. That's about it.

The Watson Wagon peels away.

SCENE 11: FINDING A BIG NEEDLE IN A BIGGER HAYSTACK

EXT. PICNIC BENCHES, BELLOWS BEACH—TEN MINUTES LATER

The girls stand on top of a picnic table under a shady tree. Noelani scans the beach while Lulu looks at her phone.

> LULU
> (reading out loud from her phone)
> "Military time is simple: 1200 hours is the same as noon. Then you add each hour"...

Pause.

> LULU
> So, let's see, 1600 would be...
> (thinks)
> ...four p.m.

Lulu grabs Noelani's arm.

> LULU
> (excitedly)
> You could see your mom in, like, three hours!

NOELANI

Let me point out, Lu: My mom's supposed to land at the Marine Corps Air Station at Kaneohe Bay. That's forty-five minutes away 'cause we're stranded here at Bellows Marine Training Area.

Lulu plunks her phone into her tote bag, then reaches in and gives the squeaky shoe a squeeze.

LULU

First things first. Let's help baby Adams. She's about to be born. It's a brand-new ohana, Noe! We're big girls. We've been daughters for eleven years! We'll worry about us and our moms next.

NOELANI
(softly)
You're right. We even promised that we'd find Colonel Adams.

Lulu and Noelani now both gaze at the beach from end to end.

CAMERA PANS THE BEACH. It's full of people sunning, tossing balls, making sand castles, or just relaxing.

NOELANI
Finding him this way isn't going to be easy.

Lulu climbs off the bench.

LULU

Exactly why we're going to have to head onto the sand ourselves.

EXT. BELLOWS BEACH SAND–CONTINUOUS

CAMERA ZOOMS IN ON Lulu. She clumsily trudges across the sand. Her hair waves wildly in the moist, salty breeze. Her face shines greasy white thanks to her sweat mingling with sunscreen. Watson, sporting his favorite orange sunglasses with fuchsia lenses, tromps along next to Lulu. Noelani wanders well behind.

LULU
(calls back to Noelani)
Still no sign of the colonel?

Noelani shakes her head.

LULU
(shouting)
Maybe he's not on the beach anymore?

Lulu slogs another few feet, then sits down. Noelani reaches Lulu and sits next to her.

LULU

I've really messed up this day, just like I ruined the whole summer.

LULU
(faces her friend)
Your mom's arriving on the other side of the island, and
you're stuck here with me. Mrs. Adams is having her
baby any minute, and I didn't tell Colonel Adams.

YAP. YAP. RUFF. RRRRUUUFFF. YAP. YAP.

Watson barks and stomps his paws along the shore, though he's
careful not to let his paws touch water.

Lulu rushes to her pug.

LULU
(looks out in the ocean)
What is it? Stay away from the water. I don't have
your floaties.

Lulu rubs the sand stuck to her arms when she spots THE
ALOHA CAP.

ANGLE: Lulu racing into the vast, blue ocean.

Lulu wades into the rolling waves, shoes and all! When she's on
her tippy toes, she ducks under the warm, turquoise water and
swims a few feet. She comes up and zeros in on THE ALOHA
hat. It's still farther out.

LULU
HEEEEYYYY! Colonel Adams!!

She waves her arms wildly.

A CRASH of salty wave water smacks Lulu in the face. She goes down from the unexpected WHACK and the sting that follows. She struggles up but instantly gets another WALLOP. Underwater, she squats into a ball and pulls herself down so that the wave doesn't tumble her along the ocean bottom.

When Lulu surfaces, water clogging her ears and salt water burning her eyes, she's dumbstruck!

The person wearing the ALOHA hat rides by on a boogie board. The person is a LITTLE GIRL about six years old. Two long, wet, black braids stick to her back. She wears a powder-blue bathing suit covered in rainbows.

ANGLE: Lulu staggers out of the water. Noelani sloshes toward her friend.

LULU

I guess the company made more than one of that ALOHA hat.

NOELANI

Don't feel too bad. Watson didn't know either.

They walk toward Watson but soon break into a RUN. A really tall, muscular man wearing an ALOHA hat has Watson over his massive shoulders and is spinning him around.

LULU

Colonel Adams?! Is that you?

COLONEL ADAMS

I was clear across the beach and all I could hear was this dog yelping his head off—

LULU

(zooming-fast talking)

Colonel Adams, sorry to interrupt you, ummm, sir. But we're looking for you. Mrs. Adams is having the baby! She asked us to tell you to, ummm, well, she said to get to the hospital "on the double."

OOOOPH. Watson thuds onto the sand. Colonel Adams starts yelling in all directions.

COLONEL ADAMS

(cupping his hands around his mouth)

HELP!! I'm having a baby! Anyone have a phone?

Noelani sprints toward Lulu's bag and in a flash hands Lulu's phone to Colonel Adams.

LULU

Excuse me, Colonel?

Colonel Adams stares at her as he punches numbers into the phone. He's now all business.

                    LULU

You know how you're having Noelani's mom come in to
take over for you?

                COLONEL ADAMS

So much for top-secret information. Yes. She's choppering
in off *USS America* right now. I'm turning over command
to her at 1600.

                    LULU

We heard. At that other marine place. What's it called, Noe?

Noelani quivers nearby but speaks up when she catches Lulu's eye.

                   NOELANI

Kaneohe Bay.

                    LULU

Yeah. And, well, I've done some math. Mrs. Adams went
off in the Watson Wagon at about 1300. We've been looking
for you for about an hour so now it's about 1400. If you
have to shower and change and get to that Kaneohe place,
you won't get to the hospital before, well, at least 1900.

Colonel Adams holds the phone away from his ear a moment
and looks at Lulu.

                    LULU

Geez peas! You could totally miss your daughter being born.

COLONEL ADAMS
(phone now down at his side)
What are you suggesting, Lulu?

LULU
Wouldn't it save almost two hours if you landed
Lieutenant Colonel Nui right here?

Colonel Adams scans the beach from under the brim of the
ALOHA hat.

COLONEL ADAMS
(shouting as a man usually in charge)
This beach is full of people! No way to put a chopper
down here!

Lulu, stung by his obvious answer, plops onto the sand,
exhausted. Her energy has sputtered out.

Noelani creeps over. She lifts her eyes from her toes to Colonel Adams.

NOELANI
(soft voice sounding firm)
But you guys are United States Marines. You can land
anywhere.

Colonel Adams pulls the phone away from his ear one more
time and stares from Noelani to Lulu and then back to Noelani.

COLONEL ADAMS
Noelani, YOU have an excellent point.

Colonel Adams takes off. He sprints toward the beach parking lot with Lulu's phone pressed to his ear.

LULU

Geez peas, Noe. That's some serious inner *koa* you have! You acted super-looper courageous just now.

NOELANI

I'm not brave. It's just we promised Mrs. Adams we'd get Colonel Adams to her.

Noelani yanks Lulu up from the sand.

NOELANI
(smiling)
Now we also get to see our moms sooner.

LULU
(not smiling)
We just got one mega-huge problem. Colonel Adams has my phone!

WIDE SHOT showing girls race up the sand.

SCENE 12: A SMALL FAVOR FOR A BIG FINISH

EXT. BELLOWS BEACH PARK—CONTINUOUS

Lulu's face is boiling and burgundy. She can barely breathe. Noelani looks confused. She has no idea what to do or where to go.

LULU
(pointing)
Look! A phone booth! Let's go.

Lulu and Noelani take off toward a dirty, neglected, old telephone booth near the beach park's picnic area.

NOELANI
Do you know how to use it?

LULU
Sure. I've seen people do it tons of times in old movies.

Lulu and Noelani squeeze into the small, grimy booth. Lulu snatches the receiver and dials Alexis's cell phone.

LULU
(into the receiver)
ALOHA? HELLLOOO!! It's me, Lulu.

The girls slam heads as they both try to put their ear to the phone receiver.

NOELANI
I don't hear anything.

LULU
(trying to keep the panic out of her voice)
Me neither. Just like a dead tone.

Lulu slams the phone back on the receiver, picks it up again, and dials, again.

LULU
(shouting)
Hello! Lex. Are you there?

NOELANI
Lu! Look on the phone. It says you need to put in money.

LULU
How much? I might have some in my tote bag.

Noelani pulls a crumpled dollar from her pocket and holds it out to Lulu.

NOELANI
Here. Have this.

Lulu tries to figure out where to stick the dollar bill. It doesn't seem to fit anywhere.

RRRRUUUUMMMM. RUUUUUUMMMMM. Military truck motors rattle the glass booth. The trucks stop a few feet away.

Twenty big and tough-looking MARINES in khaki and green camouflage uniforms move out onto the beach.

RAPPING on the phone booth door makes Lulu and Noelani JUMP. It's a MARINE SERGEANT.

> **SERGEANT**
> Excuse me, you'll have get out now. We need to secure this area.

Lulu and Noelani tumble out.

> **LULU**
> Pardon me but I need to find Colonel Adams. He has my ph—

> **SERGEANT**
> No way anyone's bothering Colonel Adams now, ma'am. He's about to land a chopper on this beach by sixteen fifteen hours.

Sergeant swaggers away.

> **NOELANI**
> Lu, how soon is that?

> **LULU**
> Not exactly sure, but soon.

The girls shuffle toward the beach parking lot, where a crowd gathers.

> **LULU**
> Now I remember! We need coins to make that phone booth work.

NOELANI
(smiling)
We'll know for next time.

Almost at the parking lot, Lulu sees it and takes off.
Noelani catches up to her.

LULU
Do you see what I see?

NOELANI
I see people everywhere. Why are we running again?

LULU
There's an ice cream truck! Those guys always have coins.

At the truck, there's a long line. Since people had to get off the beach, the ice cream truck's doing a booming business.

Lulu, hair wild; clingy wet clothes; greasy, sandy face, looks part human and part sea creature. She impulsively starts jumping and waving her arms above her head, kinda like an off-timed jumping jack.

LULU
Hey! I'm trying to get my mom her job back! She's gotta make a movie! I need some change and fast.

Everyone in line at the truck notices her, including the TEEN BOY selling the ice cream. He leans his head out the service window.

TEENAGER SELLING ICE CREAM
Sure!
(reaches behind him and jangles a box full of change)
But that's not enough to make a movie.

LULU
Well, I need to make a phone call. My friend and I tried to use that phone booth but we only had a dollar bill and—

TEENAGER SELLING ICE CREAM
You just need to make a call? Why didn't ya say so?
(reaches in his pocket)
Just use my phone.

Teenager hands it down to her.

LULU
(to Teenager in the truck)
Mahalo!

TEENAGER
Hey, always happy to lend my phone to someone making a movie!

Lulu immediately dials Alexis.

Lulu stands still while it rings. After awhile...

LULU
(yelling)
No! Lex, don't hang up!! It's not Ice Scream's a Scream calling. It's me, LULU!

SCENE 13: SEND IN THE MARINES

EXT. BELLOWS BEACH AND PARKING LOT—2:55 P.M. (or 1455 in military time)

Lulu spots Alexis's black Bug first. She swings her tote bag over her head like a lasso to stop the car.

It halts and the passenger door opens.

LULU
Aloha, Maxwell! Are my parents with you?

Lulu peers into the car.

MAXWELL
Behind us.

An exhausted-looking Maxwell pushes his moppish curly bangs off his forehead every few seconds. He has a cell phone pressed against his left ear. Alexis, wearing a navy strapless sundress with a flirty short skirt, hops out. Her silky hair shines and her red lips glisten.

MAXWELL
(looking from Lulu to Alexis)
You sisters don't look anything alike, but you are BOTH
making me crazy.

Lulu and Alexis shoot each other a quick smile.

LULU
(whispers)
Lex, you got them to come?

ALEXIS
(pointing to an Escalade behind her)
Yup. But I'm warning you. Linc is freaking and Fiona
may come out swinging a hatchet.

Noelani retreats toward the woods behind the parking lot. Lulu
runs after her.

BELLOWS PARKING LOT—CONTINUOUS

A car door clicks open.

Fiona steps out. The navy pants and stiff white blouse she's been
wearing since this morning still look fresh. Even the striped
sweater hasn't slid an inch off her thin shoulders. Her long, dark
hair, however, is now pulled back into a ponytail. Her mouth
seems held by a coil about to spring open.

FIONA
(hissing)
Maxwell. I don't see *any* aircraft of *any* kind here. I only see, ahhh, ahhh public carnival!

Fiona tugs off her sunglasses. Her narrowing eyes blaze fury. She surveys the beachgoers crowding the beach park and parking lot.

MAXWELL
(stuttering)
R-r-r-right. I s-s-see what you mean b-b-but—

Linc approaches. An olive-green messenger bag stuffed with a screenplay is slung over his shoulder.

LINC
(shouting)
I'm already reading the new script from the new director.
(pulls script from his bag and shakes it at Fiona)
For your information: I'm one of America's hottest action stars!

Linc turns back toward the Escalade.

Meanwhile, the Sound Engineer and Camera Man set up their equipment. They're not sure what's going on. Maxwell got them to head out with Fiona. He promised she was directing the end of the movie. Of course, Maxwell just did and said what Alexis told him to.

Fiona spots Maxwell.

FIONA
(seething)
I hope you like cold, wet England. You can get your bags
and leave tonight.

Fiona turns to get back into the Escalade but spins back around
to Maxwell.
(continues)
Just wondering how you could be such a daft idiot!
Making us traipse out here!

MAXWELL
Alexis said that—

Fiona turns around to see Alexis. She's furiously tugging the
ends of her long hair.

LULU
(huffing and puffing)
Hi, Mom!
(grabs her left side)
I've got a cramp. Sorry. I was trying to get Noelani to
help me explain.

FIONA
Sorry?!

LULU
I can clear things up.

Linc hurries back over when he spots Lulu.

ALEXIS
(finding her voice)
See, this morning Lulu told me—

LINC and FIONA
LULU?!!

LULU
First, don't blame Maxwell.

Maxwell's too busy pushing curls from his forehead to think of anything to say.

LULU
Lex and I—

Lulu looks at Alexis, who's cowering near Maxwell.

FIONA
(deep anger)
Alexis was also involved in this disaster?

LULU
Well...no is the answer. It really was me. She was just involved because of *koa* and *ohana*.

LINC
You're not even speaking English!

FIONA
(yelling)
We're standing in the middle of...who knows where... looking ridiculous because Maxwell insisted a special helicopter was coming to a secret spot.

Marine Sergeant 1 approaches Lulu.

SERGEANT 1
Ma'am, these are compliments of Colonel Adams.

Marine Sergeant 1 from the front gate hands Lulu binoculars. She drapes the strap around her neck.

LULU
(to her parents)
See! Maxwell's right. There will be a helicopter here.

VRRRUUUM of motors.

Television NEWS TRUCKS SCREECH into the parking lot. Camera people and reporters rush toward the sand. A woman in a frosty-pink pantsuit waves her pink nails as soon as she sees Lulu.

MRS. LYONS
(calls out to Lulu)
Helloo-ha! I told you I know everyone on the island! I got all the TV stations.

She approaches Lulu, Linc, and Fiona.

MRS. LYONS
(trills to Linc and Fiona)
Hi! You two are the only people I don't know in O'ahu. I'm
Clarissa Lyons. I looove that Lulu planned all this!

FIONA and LINC
She did?!

MRS. LYONS
So exciting. Off to get a great view! Toodles!

Mrs. Lyons dashes off to catch the news crews.

Uncle Akamu's battered blue van CHUGS around the TV vans.
Ohana kids wave little American and Hawaiian flags out the
window.

LULU
(shouts)
Aloha, you guys!

FIONA
(shrieking)
I'm all about being in control! This situation is totally
OUT of control! All I need now is that heartless, cheap,
career-killing Sanyo to see me here!

With the clamor, Fiona hadn't heard Mr. Sanyo clear his throat.
But Linc did. He taps Fiona's shoulder and points.

They turn and are face-to-face with a very angry Mr. Sanyo.

Fiona takes three practiced deep breaths and exhales slowly after each one. Linc is too stunned to do anything.

> MR. SANYO
> (glowering)
> What the—

Lulu pounces in between them. Before she can open her mouth, Noelani yanks at her shirt.

> NOELANI
> (whispering)
> Lulu, I'm so sorry. I can't find him.

Lulu squeezes her friend's arm.

> LULU
> Geez peas! When was the last time we saw him?! I can't even remember.

> NOELANI
> At the ice cream truck?

> LULU
> In the phone booth?

> LULU and NOELANI
> The beach!!

Lulu turns back to the cluster of adults.

LULU

I can explain later, but right now I've gotta get to the beach. I have a crisis.

All gape at her.

LULU

Well, I mean, another crisis.

LINC

My anger right now is way beyond—

FIONA
(harshly)
Whatever you did here today, Lulu, was unacceptable. You've ruined so much.

LULU
(looking her mother in the eye)
I didn't mean to. I wanted to do the opposite. I got the end of your movie all staged and ready. You just have to direct it.

HEAVY SILENCE.

ALEXIS

And, Fiona, if you don't get everything set and ready to roll, like, ASAP, you're going to miss your final scene!

Alexis winks at her sister.

ALEXIS
(to Lulu)
Now go find that disgusting dog of yours before it drowns
again. I'll handle this gang.

CAMERA PULLS BACK to show Fiona barking orders, Linc
and the crew scrambling, and Maxwell scurrying off.

LULU
(shouts)
MR. SAAAANYO!

As soon as he looks in Lulu's direction, she tosses him the
binoculars from around her neck. He grabs them in midair and
presses them to his eyeglasses. Alexis gives Lulu a thumbs-up.

EDGE OF BELLOWS BEACH—FIVE MINUTES LATER

OUUUU OUUUUU OUUUUU. Howling noises drift over the
noise of the waves and the blowing wind.

LULU
Oh no! That's Watson!

NOELANI
He hears the blades already.
(pointing)
Look behind that cloud!

A huge black helicopter blocks out the sun for a moment.

Twenty Marines have made a huge circle with orange flares in the sand.

LULU

(yelling to Noelani over the roar of the approaching copter)
How am I going to find puggie?

Noelani, who had been staring down at her toes, slightly lifts her head to answer.

NOELANI

I don't know.

Lulu climbs on top of a picnic table and looks around.

CAMERA SHOWS Lulu's POV. Vehicles jam the beach parking lot. Hundreds of people stand frozen. All look toward the sky. Some have climbed up on their cars. Lulu spots Uncle Akamu, Auntie Moana, and her Ohana pals sitting on the roof of the blue van. She waves, but they don't see her. Like everyone else, they're watching the sky.

One sharp voice cuts through the noise.

FIONA

The lighting is perfect right now. Roll tape!

WHIRRR WHIRRRR drowns out every other noise. The blades make more wind than the usual late-afternoon wind blowing off the Pacific Ocean.

Marine Sergeant 2 approaches. Lulu recognizes him. It's the other Sergeant from the guard gate.

SERGEANT 2
Miss Nui, come with me, please.

Noelani's eyes open wide. Shocked and scared, she blinks nervously.

NOELANI
(weakly)
Me?

LULU
Noe! It's OK. We know this guy.

Sergeant 2 stands at attention, waiting.

Lulu gives Noelani a light shove.

LULU
Go on. And look! Watson wants to go too.

Watson, who had been scrounging up food left on the beach, trots up to Sergeant 2. Memories of picnic scraps are fresh in his doggie brain. If someone's going back out on the beach, he's coming along. ·

Noelani follows Sergeant 2 onto the sand and toward the orange flares. He pauses to hand her ear protectors and sunglasses. Watson waddles behind them. Sergeant 1 halts puggie long enough to place dark-green aviator sunglasses on his face to protect his eyes.

MR. SANYO
(to Lulu)
Now this is my kinda movie!

WIDE SHOT of the massive HELICOPTER bearing down on the beach, getting closer and closer to the orange flares and fascinated onlookers.

All watch as the enormous black machine touches down on the white, powdery sand. Anyone not wearing glasses closes his or her eyes because sand flies everywhere. The roar of the whirring blades and powerful motor slowly softens.

Sergeant 2 escorts Noelani to Colonel Adams, who stands at stiff, perfect attention next to the helicopter's nose. He wears complete dress uniform, except for Lulu's ALOHA cap.

A side door swings open. A waterfall of stairs drops to the sand. Out jumps the most beautiful soldier Lulu's ever seen. Her jet-black hair is slicked back into a bun behind a cap. She wears a blue uniform with lots of pins and stripes. She swings her legs through the copter door and glides elegantly down the steep stairs as if she were a runway model. At the very last step, she turns her head toward Colonel Adams and gives him a crisp salute. He returns the salute with his right hand and, at the same time, he places his left hand on Noelani's head.

LULU
(to Mr. Sanyo)
Here comes the good part!

All watch as Lieutenant Colonel Nui walks through the sand, toward her daughter. Her crew, all wearing their dress blues, descend from the helicopter and fall in behind her.

SLOW MOTION SHOT: At about ten feet away, Noelani takes off in a run toward her mother's arms. As Noelani runs that last foot, Lieutenant Colonel Nui kneels down in the sand and folds her daughter in to her. Time seems to stop. No one talks and it feels like no one's even breathing.

HAWOOOO HAWOOOO HAWOOO!!

Everyone looks toward the old blue van. Uncle Akamu stands on the hood and blows a large, pearl-colored conch shell. It's the sound that everyone needs! Everyone cheers and claps. Old and young, men and women wipe their eyes. Parents hug their children. Children hug their parents.

Lulu feels a thin arm wrap around her waist and a kiss on the top of her damp, tangled hair.

FIONA
(choking back tears)
Lu, you make one incredible real-life director.

Linc picks Lulu up and holds her for a few moments.

LINC
(whispering into her ear)
Lu, I love you so much, but I'm gonna kill you. I'm about
to cry like a baby in front of United States Marines.

From her perch in Linc's arms, Lulu spots Colonel Adams. He
gives Lulu a salute and heads towards his jeep.

LULU
(whispering back)
Dad, don't worry, about it. The head guy, Colonel Adams,
is crying too.

SCENE 14: STARS ALL AROUND

**EXT. HARRISONS' DIAMOND HEAD ESTATE
DRIVEWAY AND FRONT ENTRANCE—5 P.M. (or 1700
military time)**

Khloe and the Cs drape beautiful, homemade leis around
the necks of the movie crew and the Marines as they come
up the Harrisons' long driveway. A huge banner that reads
"WELCOME HOME NOELANI'S MOM" hangs from a
second floor window.

Lulu spots Noelani coming up the driveway with her mom
and Tutu.

LULU
(excitedly)
Aloha! Welcome to your Welcome-Home party, Lieutenant
Colonel Nui.

LT. COLONEL NUI
Please, just call me Lea.

LULU
Mahalo, Lea. I need to borrow Noelani.
(quietly to Noelani)
C'mon. You've gotta get ready.

NOELANI
I don't think so, Lu. I can't do it.

LULU
Let's just go inside and clean up.

Lulu and Noelani look at each other in their damp, sandy, clothes, then race into the house.

INT. HARRISONS' DIAMOND HEAD ESTATE, LIVING ROOM—CONTINUOUS

Inside the wide, open living room, guests mingle. Ohana Camp kids walk around carrying trays of food they prepared all afternoon.

The house is decorated with the garden's proteas, tiare, and ilima flowers stuffed into vases with mini American and Hawaiian flags.

Lulu spots Maya next to a large orchid. She's holding a purple tray of special peanut butter sushi. Mr. Sanyo, chewing, holds a piece in his left hand and reaches for another piece with his right.

LIAM
(calls out)
Hey, Lu! Your coconut shake is a hit.

Lulu gives him a thumbs-up. She swipes a bowl of taro chips off a side table.

LULU
Noe, take that bowl of mango salsa.

NOELANI
I'm too nervous to eat anything.

LULU
(swallowing a chip)
I was thinking about my stomach, not yours. C'mon.

The girls duck and weave through the guests. They zoom up the floating staircase and down the hallway. Just before they reach Alexis's room, Noelani stops.

NOELANI
(staring at her toes)
I know I know how to hula but...but...ONLY when no one watches.

Lulu puts her arm around Noelani.

LULU

Here're two reasons you're gonna be able to do it. One, Khloe and the Cs are gonna perform with you, so you won't be up there alone.

NOELANI
(looks at Lulu)
They are? They'd dance with *me*?

LULU

And second, if you don't get up there and hula, I'm gonna do it instead.

NOELANI

You're joking, right?

LULU
(stares deep into her friend's eyes)
Nope. I am not.

NOELANI
(shock in her voice)
You'd try and dance in front of all these people?

Lulu shuffles, shakes, and slides in her disjointed and uncoordinated unique style.

LULU

I'll get Alexis to tape it. We'll call it *Hilarious Hula: Part Two.*

She steps, hops, and whirls. Lulu dances like she's telling the story of a tree thrashing about in a windstorm.

> **LULU**
> I wonder if your mom will think I'm good?

Alexis's door whips open.

> **ALEXIS**
> Lulu, you're pathetic at hula. Now, let's get glamming! Where've you been?

Khloe and the Cs race down the hall.

> **KHLOE**
> Noelani! You're gonna lead us in *Ka wailele o Nu'uanu*!

> **NOELANI**
> (shyly to Khloe)
> You'd dance with me?

> **KHLOE**
> (looks straight at Noelani)
> It would be soooo amazing if you'd even let us dance with YOU. Every kid on O'ahu knows you're THE BEST hula dancer on our island.

> **LULU**
> So, Noelani, you'll do it?

ALL look at her.

                    NOELANI
I'll try anything to keep Lulu from dancing hula in front
of my mom.

The girls jumble into Alexis's room. Her door slams shut.

EXT. SANDY BEACH IN FRONT OF THE HARRISONS' ESTATE—6 P.M. (or 1800 in military time)

The scent of mimosa flowers and orange blossoms mixes with
warm, salty sea breezes. The air smells pure Hawaii! Tiki
torches blaze. A bonfire burns. Caridyn and Maleko softly
beat *pahu* drums. Uncle Akamu and Liam strum ukuleles.
Auntie Moana begins a low, beautiful chant that floats
through the air along with the lapping waves. A hush falls
over all the guests.

Linc Harrison, the natural performer, walks up to an open area
near a bonfire.

                    LINC
For all of you who are here and want to kill me or my
wife, Fiona...
                    (pause)
...I don't blame you.

Guests chuckle. Mr. Sanyo, who has actually taken his suit
jacket off, laughs the loudest.

                    LINC
But before you do, all of you should know that this

has been the best and craziest summer because of my daughter Lu—

HUUUGH HUUUGH HUUUGH. Loud retching interrupts Linc.

All eyes turn toward the noise. It's Watson throwing up everything! Chunks of *laulau*, flecks of taro chips, hunks of mango salsa, and bits of blue, salty, plum lollipop come up in a warm gel of coconut milkshake. He retches a few feet away from Linc.

Lulu pushes her way through the guests toward Watson.

LULU
(muttering)

Geez peas! Sorry. I've gotta bury the barf in sand before he eats it.

By the time Lulu reaches Watson, Kenna and Kapono are already there.

KENNA
(whispering to Lulu)

We'll bury the barf for you.

KAPONO

Yeah. You get the show going.

LULU

Mahalo, you guys.

Lulu stands in front of the bonfire. She spots Fiona talking to Lieutenant Colonel Nui.

LULU
(top of her voice)
Aloha, everyone! Ummm, I wanted to say: Welcome home to Noelani's mom.

GUESTS
ALOHA! Welcome home!

LULU
And, also...
(pauses)
...I want to say: welcome home to my own mom. You've pretty much finished shooting *Seas the Day*.

Cast and crew in the audience CLAP wildly.

LULU
So, please...
(blinks back a tear)
...let's be a family and start summer vacation together all over again.

Everyone WHISTLES, CHEERS, and PUMPS the air.

LULU
As a present to the moms, I present a hula called *Ka wailele o Nu'uanu* about a magically beautiful waterfall that's right here on O'ahu.

The strumming, chanting, and drumming get louder. Noelani leads Khloe and the Cs out into the open circle in front of the bonfire. They wear white bikini tops and yellow sarong bottoms except Noelani, who wears an all-white sarong with ti leaves around her skirt.

The slow, beautiful song starts while the girls remain for a few beats in their starting hula position. They stand with knees slightly bent and their feet in a pie shape.

Soon they begin to *kaholo*, and their feet move right together and tap, then left together and tap. The *'ami*, the sway, comes in and all the girls have mastered the art of separating themselves the waist up from the waist down.

The *hela* move comes in with a soft forward-and-back sway. Their arms tell the story of the breathtaking waterfall. Noelani's gentle, floating, gliding arms lead. From her narrow shoulders to the tips of her slender fingers, the waterfall appears flowing, falling, and bubbling.

All the guests, hardly moving and barely breathing, watch. Everyone is captivated by the rolling waves, the shimmering moonlight, the gleaming starlight, the enchanting music, and, most of all, by the girls telling a story through a magical dance.

When the music stops, Noelani stands still, facing the ocean, arms raised high and fingertips toward the stars. The guests remain still, awed by the beauty. They follow Noelani's fingers up to the heavens and see—A SHOOTING STAR!

> LULU
> (calls out)

Hey look!

It streaks through the velvet-black sky for a moment, and then it's gone.

While everyone continues to stare into the sky, Lulu runs toward Noelani, but she's not the first to reach her. Lieutenant Colonel Nui holds her daughter tightly and rests her chin on top of Noelani's head.

> LULU
> (backing up)

Oh sorry. I'll just—

> LT. COLONEL NUI
> (releasing Noelani)

Lulu! Glad you're here. I want you to know that my life is full of adventure and rewards and—

> LULU
> (looks at the left side of her uniform)

And medals.

> LT. COLONEL NUI
> (smiling)

Yes, and medals. But I've never had an honor as great as watching my daughter dance tonight. *Mahalo* for all you did to make that happen.
> (pauses for a deep breath)

Now I'm going to walk away before this Marine mama sheds a few joyful tears.

Lulu and Noelani link arms and head down the sand. Before they reach the white ocean foam, they walk by two people cuddling. Lulu stops. She and Noelani turn around.

LULU

Lex? Is that you?

ALEXIS

Oh, hi! I mean, *Aloha*. I was just telling Max—

MAXWELL

That was gorgeous, Noelani. Totally brilliant.

Knowing Noelani isn't ready to chat quite yet, Lulu jumps in.

LULU

I knew she'd be amazing! Just like I knew we'd get summer back as a family.

ALEXIS

I gotta hand it to ya, Lu. Sometimes you get the script just right.

LULU
(tossing her arm around Noelani and Alexis)
And sometimes, I just direct the script exactly the way I want the ending to be!

FADE TO BLACK

EPILOGUE: LULU'S WRAP-UP

Before I tell you what happened the rest of my summer in Honolulu, which is lots of big stuff, I want you to know the three most important Hawaiian words I'll always remember. If I go back to L.A. and never forget these three words, I'll feel like a new, more grown-up Lulu.

ME

The first word is *koa*. It means "bravery" or "courage." When summer started, I planned to just spend time with my family and meet new friends. I wanted to chop, mince, dice, cut, and, most of all, taste new foods. I set out to touch, smell, see, and help save different plants, trees, animals, and fish. I never wanted to cause any trouble for my parents or for anyone else. But when *Seas the Day* ran into trouble, I summoned up *koa* to find ways to try and help. And when my mom got fired, my courage really kicked in. Of course, it's not easy for an eleven-year-old kid to patch up a 150 million dollar movie. Most of the brave stuff I tried created disasters. But I learned that *koa* is catching and that it's something that can be shared. So, remember, don't keep your *koa* to yourself.

MY FAMILY

The next word is *aloha*. It's easy to think you know this word. It's used for "hello" and "good-bye." It's like everyone knows the words "mom" and "dad." But *aloha*, like mom and dad, has deeper meanings, like love, kindness, tenderness, and harmony. In Honolulu, my parents found out that being called "mom" and "dad" means more than racing past their kids or scheduling slivers of time to be a family. What they really learned was a little *aloha*!

Auntie Moana and Uncle Akamu talk about the "Spirit of *aloha*." They say it's a way of living and treating each other with love and respect. They say when you live in the spirit of *aloha,* you create positive feelings that spread to others. Well, my sister, Alexis got washed up in *aloha* spirit. Her coming through for me all summer long, even when she knew I could get her in whopper tons of trouble, made her beauty on the outside match her beauty on the inside. And you know what? I'm pretty sure her boyfriend, Maxwell, liked her way better knowing that she had a little sister who she'd never let down. It showed him that she thought about more than just herself.

REAL, NEW LULU

Here's THE word that defines the new Lulu: *ohana*. The exact meaning is "family" but not just a mom, dad, and kids. *Ohana* can be grandparents, aunties, uncles, cousins, and, of course, friends. The Hawaiian spirit of *ohana* taught me that love and care bind families together and, also, knit together people, whether they are like or different from you.

Now I've gotta tell you some real *ohana* things that happened the rest of my summer in Honolulu:

1. Colonel Adams made it to the hospital to be with Mrs. Adams when their baby was born. They named her Noa Adams. It's a really cool name because *Noa* means "freedom" in Hawaiian. Noa's head already sprouted red hair like her mother's. James and I visited Noa and Mrs. Adams. Colonel Adams came in while we were there and gave me back my iPhone. He wouldn't give me back my ALOHA cap, though. He said it's now his lucky cap.

2. Noelani belonged at the best hula school on O'ahu, but Tutu and her mom didn't have the extra time or money to enroll her. Also, it might have been too scary for Noelani to do an audition. So, Khloe and the Cs and I decided to have a chat with the head *kumu* (teacher) at Island School of Hula. I played the Big Cheese Teacher a video I once took of Noelani practicing when she didn't know I was watching. And guess what? The head of the school offered Noelani a scholarship! Right then and there! So I handed the *kumu* my phone, and Khloe dialed Noelani. We put the phone on speaker and all told her together. Well, Noe's been performing as the front-and-center dancer with Island School of Hula ever since.

3. Mrs. Lyons really did know everyone on O'ahu. She wasn't just saying it. And she really wanted to be involved with movies. So, Lex and I arranged a swap-a-roo. We got her Maxwell's job as a production assistant on *Seas the Day* and Maxwell drives around Honolulu with Alexis, dropping off kids at Ohana Camp. Sometimes he just reads on mall

benches and waits for Alexis to buy new bikinis. He says he's trying to teach Lex that "a good book is mind candy." Turns out Maxwell is happier reading Shakespeare than raking sand for actors about to shoot beach scenes.

And, as you might guess, Mr. Sanyo rehired my mom to finish directing her movie. In fact, he arranged for my mom to make a sequel!! So, there's gonna be *Seas the Day II* next summer. The first thing Mom did was hire Dad to star in the new one. The second thing she did was invite all my pals to be movie extras. But, best of all, she hired Auntie Moana, Uncle Akamu, and Caridyn to make the movie's soundtrack! So, it just goes to show what deep *koa*, *aloha* spirit, *ohana* feelings, and peanut butter sushi can do.

Acknowledgments

Thank you to my incredible O'ahu research team: Debbie, Eliana, and Kiara Berger-Reeves.

Thank you to my unbelievable Hawaiian tutor: Caridyn Colburn.

Thank you to my remarkable reader (250 pages in one night): Virginia Beutner.

About the Author

Elisabeth Wolf is a bit Lulu. She lives in Los Angeles, where she grows fruits, vegetables, and native flowers. She bakes her children's birthday cakes and eats spicy Mexican food. Each year for summer vacation, she makes her husband, children, and dog move to Maine, where they explore coves, gaze at tall trees, and hunt for sand dollars. Most of all, they laugh with friends and spend time as a family. But make NO mistake: she loves slipping into town for some fun shopping and a good pedicure. *Lulu in Honolulu* is her second book.